RUTHLESSLY
BEDDED BY
THE ITALIAN
BILLIONAIRE

RUTHLESSLY BEDDED BY THE ITALIAN BILLIONAIRE

BY

EMMA DARCY

MILLS & BOON®

Pure reading pleasure™

First published in Great Britain 2008
Large Print edition 2009
Harlequin Mills & Boon Limited,
Eton House, 18-24 Paradise Road,
Richmond, Surrey TW9 1SR

© Emma Darcy 2008

ISBN: 978 0 263 20570 1

Set in Times Roman 16½ on 21 pt.
16-0309-44454

Printed and bound in Great Britain
by CPI Antony Rowe, Chippenham, Wiltshire

CHAPTER ONE

Sydney, Australia

'Miss Rossini…'

Another voice calling to her, using Bella's name.

Jenny struggled to understand. Her mind felt weirdly disconnected, taking in only snatches of what was said. She couldn't make sense of what she heard. It was as if she was locked inside a fog that almost cleared sometimes but then swallowed her up into a blank nothingness. Was this a nightmare that kept coming and receding? She needed to wake up, get a grip on what was real, but her eyelids were so heavy.

'Miss Rossini…'

There it was again. Where was Bella? Why did the voices use her friend's name as though it belonged to her? It was wrong. Her head ached with trying to figure it out. The fog swirled. So much easier to slide back into oblivion where there was no painful confusion. Yet she wanted answers, wanted the torment of this nightmare to end. Which meant focusing all the energy she could summon on opening her eyes.

'Oh, dear God! She woke up! She's awake!'

The screech hurt her ears. The sudden glare of light made her want to close her eyes, but she fought the impulse, frightened of losing the strength to open them again. Her blurred vision picked up a flurry of movement.

'I'll get the doctor!'

Doctor…white bed…white screens…tubes stuck in her arm. This had to be a hospital. Some kind of sling was on her other arm. She couldn't see her legs. The blanket on the bed was covering them. She tried to move them but couldn't manage it. Dead weight. Her mind filled with a galloping fear. Was she paralysed?

A nurse appeared at the foot of her bed, a pretty blond woman with anxious blue eyes. 'Hi! My name is Alison. I've paged Dr Farrell. He'll be here in a minute, Miss Rossini.'

Jenny tried to say that wasn't her name but her mouth wouldn't co-operate. Her lips, her throat were so dry they felt cracked.

'I'll get you a cup of ice,' Alison said, darting away.

When she returned she was accompanied by a man who introduced himself as Dr Farrell. Alison fed her a piece of ice which she rolled around her tongue, working moisture from it, grateful for the lubrication trickling down her throat.

'Glad to have you with us at last, Miss Rossini,' the doctor was saying, looking cheerful about it. He was a short stocky man, probably mid-thirties, dark hair given a buzz cut that seemed to defy the receding hairline, certainly no vanity about hiding it. His bright brown eyes twinkled approval of her wakeful state. 'You've been in a coma for the past two weeks.'

Why? What's wrong with me? Panic churned through her as she tried to telegraph the questions with her eyes.

'You were in a car accident,' he said, understanding her need to know. 'For some reason you were not wearing a seat belt and you were thrown clear of the wreck. However, you suffered a severe concussion, and the bruising of the brain undoubtedly contributed to the coma. You also had three broken ribs, a broken arm, deep lacerations on one leg and you have a cast on the other, fixing up a broken ankle. However, you are mending nicely and it's only a matter of time before you'll be on your feet again.'

Relief whooshed through her. She wasn't paralysed. However, her bruised brain wasn't working so well. It couldn't recollect any memory of a car accident. Besides, it didn't make sense that she hadn't been wearing a seat belt. She always did. It was an automatic action whenever she got into a car.

'I see you frowning, Miss Rossini. Are you up to speaking yet?' the doctor asked kindly.

I'm not Bella. Why didn't they know that?

She licked her lips and managed to croak, 'My name…'

'Good! You know your name.'

No!

She tried again. 'My friend…'

The doctor sighed, grimaced. His eyes softened with sympathy. 'I'm sorry to tell you that your friend passed away in the accident. Nothing could be done for her. The car burst into flames before help arrived. If you had not been thrown clear…'

Bella…dead? Burnt? The horror of it brought a gush of tears. The doctor took her hand and patted it, mouthing words of comfort, but Jenny didn't really hear anything but the tone. All she could think of was that being burned was a terrible way to die and Bella had been so kind to her, taking her in, giving her a place to live, even letting her borrow her name so she could work at the Venetian Forum since everyone employed there had to be Italian. Or of Italian heritage.

Was that how their identities had got mixed up?

The tears kept coming. The doctor left, appointing the nurse to sit at her bedside and talk to her. Jenny couldn't speak. She was too overwhelmed by the shock of her situation and the dreadful loss of her friend. Her only friend. And Bella had had no one, either. No family. Both of them orphans—a bond that had given them immediate empathy with each other.

Who would bury her? What would happen to her apartment and all her things…the home she'd made, waiting for her to come back… except she never would return to it.

Eventually the exhaustion of grief drew her into sleep.

Another nurse had replaced Alison when she woke up.

'Hello. My name is Jill,' she said encouragingly. 'Can I get you anything, Miss Rossini?'

Not Rossini. Kent. Jenny Kent. But there was no one to care about who or what she was now that Bella was gone.

Fear speared through the dark turmoil in her mind.

Where would she go when they finally released her from this hospital? Social Services would probably find some place for her, as they had throughout her childhood and early teenage years—places she'd hated—and if she was forced back into the welfare system because of her injuries, that sleazy abusive creep might hear of it.

Revulsion cramped her stomach. The officials hadn't believed her when she had reported their highly experienced social worker for *helping* down-and-out girls in return for sexual favours.

He was too entrenched in the system not to be trusted, and the other girls had been too frightened of his vengeful power to back up her report. She'd been painted as a vindictive liar for not getting what she wanted from him, and no doubt he would revel in victimising her again if he became aware of her present circumstances.

Yet what other choice was viable? Simply to survive she would have to be dependent on welfare until she could stand on her own two feet again and make her way, selling her sketches on the street as she had before meeting Bella. Impossible to stay on at the Venetian Forum without the Rossini name.

The wild thought flashed into her mind—did she have to give it up?

Everyone thought Jenny Kent was dead.

There was no one to care if she was, no one to come forward to claim her. If officialdom believed she was Isabella Rossini…if she found out why they did…would it be too terrible of her to take over her friend's identity for a while…stay in the apartment…go on working at the Venetian Forum…build up some savings…give herself time to think, to plan out what to do when she felt up to coping on her own?

Wouldn't her friend have wanted that for her instead of all of it just…*ending*?

CHAPTER TWO

Rome, Italy
Six Months Later

DANTE Rossini unwound himself from Anya's voluptuous charms and reached for his cell-phone.

'Don't!' she snapped. 'You can pick up the message later.'

'It's my grandfather,' he said, ignoring the protest.

'Oh, fine! He calls and you jump!'

Her burst of petulance annoyed him. He sliced her a quelling look as he flipped open the cell-phone, knowing it could only be his grandfather because no one else had been given this private number—an immediate link between them. He'd bought the phone for this specific use when Nonno had been diagnosed with inoperable cancer, and yes, he was ready to jump whenever it rang. Three months at most, the doctors had forecast, and already a month had gone by. Time was running out for Marco Rossini.

'Dante here,' he said quickly, aware of a tight knot of urgency in his chest. 'What can I do for you, Nonno?'

Frustrated that her jeering words had had no effect on him, Anya flounced off the bed and strutted angrily towards the bathroom. Time was running out on Anya Michaelson, too, he decided. She always expected to be indulged, which he hadn't minded in the past, given her fantastic body and her talent for erotic games, but her self-centred core was beginning to irritate him.

He heard his grandfather wheezing, gathering breath enough to speak. 'It's a family matter, Dante.'

Family? Usually it was a business issue he wanted resolved. 'What's the problem?' he asked.

'I'll explain when you get here.'

'You want me to come now?'

'Yes. No time to waste.'

'I'll be there before lunch,' he promised.

'Good boy!'

Boy... Dante smiled ironically as he flicked the cell-phone shut. He was thirty years old, already designated to take over the management of a global business, having met every challenge his grandfather had set for him from his teenage years onward. Only Marco Rossini had the balls to still call him a boy, and Dante excused it as a term of familial affection. He'd just turned six years old when his parents were killed in a speed-boat accident and he'd been his grandfather's *boy* ever since.

'What about me?' Anya demanded as he rose from the bed.

She'd propped herself provocatively against

the bathroom doorjamb, every lush naked curve jutting out at him, her long blond hair arranged in tousled disarray over her shoulders, her full-lipped mouth pouting. The desire she'd stirred earlier was gone. The only feeling she raised now was impatience.

'I'm sorry. I have to leave.'

'You promised to take me shopping today.'

'Shopping is unimportant.'

She was blocking the way into the bathroom. He took hold of her waist to move her aside. She flung her arms around his neck, pressing herself against him, her green eyes sparking anger. 'It is not unimportant to me, Dante. You promised…'

'Another time, Anya. I'm needed on Capri. Now, let go.'

His voice was cold. His eyes were cold. She let go, infuriated by his command but obeying it. He stepped past her and walked into the shower stall, not glancing back.

'I hate the way you switch off!' she screeched. 'I hate it!'

'Then find yourself another man, Anya,' he said carelessly and turned on the water, drowning out any extraneous noise. The last thing he wanted was to be subjected to a hissy fit, and he didn't really care if Anya found herself another man. Let someone else buy her clothes and jewellery for the pleasure of her body. There were always other beautiful women, eager to share his bed.

She was gone when he emerged from the bathroom and he didn't give her another thought. As he plunged into the business of getting ready to leave—calling the helicopter pilot to be on standby for a flight to Capri, dressing, grabbing some breakfast—his mind was sifting through the family positions, trying to work out who was causing his grandfather concern.

Uncle Roberto was currently in London, overseeing the refurbishing of the hotel, happily immersing himself in the kind of creativity he loved. He'd always managed his *gay* life with discretion and Marco tolerated his son's homosexuality, with the proviso that it wasn't paraded under his nose. Had something *unacceptable* happened?

Aunt Sophia had shed her third money-sucking husband a year ago, at the cost of several million dollars, causing Marco to gnash his teeth over his wayward daughter's total lack of judgement. She had married in turn an American evangelist, a Parisian playboy and an Argentinian polo player, all of whom apparently exuded enough sexual charisma to woo and win themselves a very wealthy wife. Had she started another unsuitable liaison?

Then there was his cousin, Lucia, Aunt Sophia's twenty-four-year-old daughter by the Parisian playboy, a sly little minx whom he'd never liked. Even as a child she'd had a habit of spying on people and tattling if she thought it would win her some advantage. But she was always sweetness itself to Marco. Dante couldn't imagine *her* giving their grandfather a problem. Lucia would avoid that like the plague, especially when there was a hefty inheritance in sight.

Marco himself had only married once. His wife had died before Dante was born, and Marco had satisfied himself with a string of mistresses over the years. They'd been treated well and paid off handsomely at the end of each 'arrangement.' None of them should be causing trouble.

Mulling over the possibilities was probably pointless, though Dante liked to be mentally prepared to carry out any directive his grandfather gave. Marco had drilled into him that knowledge was power. Anyone who was surprised at an important meeting had not done their homework and was instantly at a disadvantage. Dante was rarely surprised these days. Though he had been surprised by his grandfather's choice to spend his last months at the villa on Capri.

Why not the palazzo in Venice? The worldwide chain of Gondola Hotels, the Venetian Forums built in 'little Italy' sections of major cities…all were inspired by the place Marco called home. Of course, the air in Venice was not as sweet as on the island, the view not as clean, the sunshine not so accessible, not for a very sick man. Still, his grandfather had been born in Venice and Dante had expected him to want to die there.

He wondered again about that choice as the helicopter flew him towards Capri. His gaze swept around the high grey cliffs dotted with scrubby trees, the rocky outcrops spearing up from the sea, the predominantly white township sprawling around the top edge of the island, the water below a brilliant turquoise blue. There was nothing even faintly reminiscent of Venice.

The villa had always been a holiday place, mostly used by Aunt Sophia and Uncle Roberto. Dante had spent some of his school vacations there but his grandfather had only ever dropped in on them, not staying for long, certainly not ever demonstrating a fondness for the relaxed lifestyle it offered. He'd always seemed impatient to be gone about his business again.

The helicopter landed on the rear terrace of the villa grounds. It was almost noon and the sun was hot enough for Dante to be glad to reach the flag-stoned walkway, which was well shaded by pine trees and the profusion of bougainvillea spread over the columned pergola. He was not so glad to see Lucia at the other end of it, walking out to meet him.

She favoured her father in looks, more French than Italian, dark-brown hair cut in a very chic bob, her fine-boned face featuring a straight elegant nose, a full-lipped sensual mouth, bright brown eyes that were always keenly observant. She wore a coquettish, little-girl dress that shouted French designer class, geometrically patterned in brown and white and black, the miniskirt showing off her long slim legs.

'Nonno is in the front courtyard, waiting for you,' she said, turning to accompany him as he came level with her.

'Thank you. No need for you to escort me, Lucia.'

She stuck to his side. 'I want to know what's going on.'

'He called me, not you.'

She flashed him a resentful look. 'I'm just as much *family* as you, Dante.'

She'd eavesdropped on the call. He kept walking, saying nothing for her to get her teeth into. They entered the villa, moving towards the atrium, a central gathering place that connected the wings spreading out from it and led to the front courtyard.

Frustrated by his silence, Lucia offered information to tempt some speculation. 'A man came yesterday afternoon. He didn't give a name. He brought a briefcase with him and had a private meeting with Nonno. It left Nonno looking even more ill. I'm worried about him.'

'I'm sure you're doing your best to brighten him up, Lucia,' he said blandly.

'If I know what the problem is…'

'I have no idea.'

'Don't play dumb with me, Dante. You always have an idea.' The bite in her voice softened to a sweet wheedle. 'I just want to help. Whatever Nonno heard from that man yesterday has knocked the life out of him. It's awful seeing him so sunk into himself.'

Bad news, Dante thought, steeling himself to deal with the fallout as best he could. 'I'm sorry to hear it,' he said, 'but I can't tell you what I don't know, Lucia. You'll have to wait until Nonno chooses to reveal what's on his mind.'

'You'll tell me after you've talked with him?' she pressed.

He shrugged. 'Depends on whether it's confidential or not.'

'I'm the one here looking after him. I need to know.'

His grandfather had a private nurse and a

whole body of servants looking after him. He shot his cousin a mocking look. 'You're here looking after your own interests, Lucia. Let's not pretend otherwise.'

'Oh, you…you…' Her mouth clamped down on whatever epithet she would have liked to fling at him.

It was clear to Dante she hated him for seeing through her artifices, always had, but open enmity was not her game.

'I love Nonno and he loves me,' she stated tightly. 'You might do well to remember that, Dante.'

An empty threat, but it probably gave her some satisfaction to leave him with it. They'd reached the atrium and she sheered off to the right, probably heading for the main entertainment room from where she could view what went on in the courtyard, though she wouldn't be able to hear what was said.

Dante continued on, only pausing when he stepped outside, taking in the scene before announcing his arrival. His grandfather was resting in a well-cushioned chaise lounge, his face shaded by an umbrella, the rest of his brutally wasted body soaking up the natural warmth of the sun.

He wore navy silk pyjamas, their looseness emphasising rather than hiding the loss of his once powerful physique. His eyes were closed. Sunken cheeks made his cheekbones too prominent, his proud Roman nose too big, but there was still an indomitable air about his jutting chin. His skin had tanned, probably from many mornings spent like this. It made his thick, wavy hair look shockingly whiter.

The nurse sat on a chair beside him, ready to attend to his every need. She was reading a book. A pitcher of fruit juice and a set of glasses stood on a table within easy reach. Tubs of flowers provided pleasing cascades of colour, and the brilliant blue vista of sea and sky generated a peaceful ambience. But Dante knew the sense of peace had to be a lie. Something was wrong and he had to fix it.

His footsteps on the terrace flagstones as he moved forward alerted the nurse to his presence, and his grandfather's eyelids snapped open. The nurse rose to her feet. His grandfather directed a dismissive wave at her and gestured for Dante to take the chair she had vacated. He didn't speak until she had gone and his grandson was settled close to him. Greetings were unnecessary and any inquiry about his health was unwelcome, so Dante waited in silence to hear what he'd been summoned to hear.

'I have kept many things from you, Dante. Private things, Personal things. Painful things.' A rueful grimace expressed his grandfather's reluctance to confide them. 'Now is the time to tell you.'

'As you wish, Nonno,' Dante said quietly, not liking the all too evident distress.

The usually bright dark eyes were clouded as his grandfather bluntly stated, 'Your grandmother, the only woman I ever really loved, my beautiful Isabella, died in this villa.'

His voice faltered, choked with emotion. Dante waited for him to recover, feeling oddly embarrassed by so much feeling, never openly expressed before. The only knowledge he'd had of his grandmother was the occasional reference in newspapers of Marco's one and only wife having died of a drug overdose. It had happened before he was born, and when he'd queried the story, his grandfather had vehemently forbidden any further mention of it.

Dante had privately assumed he had felt some guilt over his wife's untimely and scandalous death, but given she was the only woman he had ever really loved, perhaps there had been a deep and abiding grief that he couldn't bear to touch upon. It did answer why Marco had chosen to die here, too.

A deep sigh ended in another grimace. 'We had a third son.'

The missing Rossini 'wild child'—another sensational story occasionally popping up in newspapers, full of lurid speculation about the rebellious black sheep who'd obviously refused to knuckle under to what Marco wanted of him, dropping completely out of his father's world— speculation that was never answered by the Rossinis—a family skeleton kept so firmly in the cupboard, Dante's curiosity about the uncle he'd never known had always been frustrated. His jerk of surprise at the totally unexpected opening of this door evoked a sharply dismissive gesture from his grandfather, demanding forebearance.

'Just listen.' The command held no patience for questions. 'I banished Antonio from our lives. No one in the family was to even speak his name. Because of him, my Isabella died. He killed his mother, not deliberately, but he gave her the designer drug that led to her death. It was *his* fault and I couldn't forgive him.'

Dante's mind reeled with shock. It took him several moments to attach some current significance to the revelations of this traumatic family history. Had his exiled uncle resurfaced? Was this the problem?

'He was the youngest of our four children. Your father, Alessandro—' his grandfather sighed, shaking his head, still grieved by the loss of his eldest son '—he was my boy in every way. As you are, Dante.'

Yes, Dante thought. Even in looks, both he and his father had inherited Marco's thick wavy hair, his deeply set dark-chocolate eyes, strong Roman nose, and the slight cleft centring their squarish chins.

'Roberto…he was softer,' his grandfather went on in a tone of rueful reminiscence. 'It was obvious from early on he would not be a competitor like Alessandro, but he does well enough with his artistic talent. And Sophia, our first girl…we spoilt her, gave her too much, indulged her every whim. I cannot really blame her for the behaviour I now have to pay for. Then came Antonio…'

His eyes closed, as though the memory of his youngest son was still cloaked in darkness. It took a visible effort to speak of him. 'He was a very bright child, mischievous, merry, given to creating amusing mayhem. He made us laugh. Isabella adored him. Of our four children, he looked most like her. He was…her joy.'

Dante heard the pain in every word and knew that Marco had shared his wife's joy in the boy.

'School was too easy for him. He wasn't challenged enough. He looked for other excitement, adventures, parties, physical thrills, experimenting with drugs. I didn't know about the drugs, but Isabella did. She kept it from me. When she died, Antonio confessed that she had been trying to make him stop and he had urged her to try the drug, to see for herself how marvellous it would make her feel and how completely harmless it was.'

His eyes opened and black derision flashed from them as he bitterly repeated, 'Harmless…'

'Tragic,' Dante murmured, imagining the horror of discovering how his wife's death had occurred, and the double grief his grandfather had suffered.

'Antonio should have died, not my Isabella. So I made him dead as far as my world was concerned.'

Dante nodded sympathetic understanding. None of this had touched his life and he still felt somewhat stunned that so much had been kept totally suppressed by the family. No doubt it was a measure of his grandfather's dominating and singularly ruthless power that not one word of the mother/son drug connection had leaked out, not privately nor publicly.

A mirthless little laugh gravelled from his grandfather's throat. His eyes seemed to mock himself as he said, 'I thought I might make peace with him. It's bad enough for any man to have one son die before him. Losing Alessandro was…but at least I had you, my son's son, filling that gap. Antonio was completely lost. And *is* completely lost. There can be no making peace with him.'

Dante frowned. 'Do you mean…?'

'I hired a firm of private investigators to find him, bring me news of the life he'd made for himself, information that would tell me if it was viable to set up a meeting between us. The owner of the firm called on me yesterday. Antonio and his wife died in a plane crash two years ago—a small private plane he was flying himself. Bad weather, pilot error…'

'I'm sorry, Nonno.'

'Too late for making peace,' he muttered. 'But he did leave a daughter, Dante. A daughter whom he named Isabella, after his mother, and I want you to fly to Australia and bring her here to me.' His eyes suddenly blazed with a concentration of life. 'I want *you* to do it, Dante, because I know you'll do everything in your power to make her come with you. And there is so little time…'

'Of course I'll do it for you, Nonno. Do you know where she is?'

'Sydney.' His mouth twisted with irony. 'She even works in the Venetian Forum we built there. You will have no trouble finding her.' He leaned over, picked up a manila folder which was lying on the low table beside his chaise. 'All the information you need is in here.'

He held it out and Dante took it.

'Isabella Rossini…' The name rolled off his grandfather's tongue in a tone of deep longing. 'Bring Antonio's daughter home to me, Dante. My Isabella would have wished it. Bring our grand-daughter home.…'

CHAPTER THREE

SATURDAY was always the best day for Jenny at the Venetian Forum. It had a carnival atmosphere with weekend crowds flocking to the morning markets set up on either side of the canal, staying on for lunch at the many restaurants bordering the main square. In their stroll around the stalls, people invariably paused to watch her drawing her charcoal portraits, many tempted to get one done of themselves or their children. She made enough money on Saturday to live on the entire week.

It was even better when it was sunny like today. Although it was only the beginning of September—the start of spring—it almost felt like summer, no clouds in the brilliant blue sky, no chilly wind, just lovely mild warmth that everyone could bask in while they looked at the marvellous array of Venetian masks, original jewellery, hand-painted scarves, individually blown-glass works of art—so many beautiful things to buy. The photographer was busy, too, taking shots of people on the Bridge of Sighs, or on their gondola rides. He wasn't in competition with her. Hand-drawn portraits were different.

She finished one of a little boy, pocketed her fee from the pleased parents, then set herself up for the next subject in line, a giggly teenage girl who was pushed onto the posing chair by a couple of equally giggly girlfriends.

A really striking man stood to one side of them. Was he waiting his turn in the chair? Jenny hoped so. He had such a handsome face, framed by a luxuriant head of hair, many shades of brown—from caramel to dark chocolate—running through its gleaming thickness, and per-fectly cut to show off its natural waves. It was a pity she couldn't capture the colours in a charcoal portrait, but his face alone presented a fascinating challenge; the sharply angled arch of his eyebrows, the deeply set eyes, the strong lines of his nose and jaw with the intriguing contrast of rather full, sensual lips and a soft dimple centred at the base of his chin.

She kept sneaking glances at him as she sketched the girl's portrait. He didn't move away, apparently content to linger and observe her working. A very masculine man, she thought, taller than most and with a physique that seemed to radiate power.

He was dressed in expensive clothes, a good quality white shirt with a thin fawn stripe and well-cut fawn slacks. The fawn leather loafers on his feet looked like Italian designer shoes. A brown suede jacket was casually slung over one shoulder. She guessed his age at about thirty, mature enough to have made his mark in some successful business, and carrying the confidence of being able to achieve anything he wanted.

Definitely a class act, Jenny decided, and wondered if he was idling away some time before a luncheon date, probably at the most expensive restaurant in the forum. It was almost noon. She half-expected some beautiful woman to appear and pluck him away. Which would be disappointing, but people like him weren't usually interested in posing for a street artist.

Gradually it sank in that he was studying her, not how she worked. It was weird, being made to feel an object of personal interest to this man. She caught his gaze roving around the chaotic volume of her dark curly hair, assessing the features of her face, which to her mind were totally unremarkable, skating down her loose black tunic and slacks to the shabby but comfortable black walking shoes she'd been wearing since breaking her ankle.

Hardly a bundle of style, she thought, wishing he'd stop making her self-conscious. She tried to block him out, concentrating on finishing the portrait of the teenager. Despite keeping her focus on her subject, her awareness of him did not go away. He remained a dominating presence on the periphery of her vision, moving purposefully to centre stage and taking the chair vacated by the teenager as the sale of the completed portrait was being transacted.

Jenny took a deep breath before resuming her own seat. Her nerves had gone all edgy, which was ridiculous. She'd wanted to draw this man, he was giving her the opportunity. Yet her hand was slightly tremulous as she picked up a fresh stick of charcoal, and the blank page on the easel suddenly seemed daunting. She had to steel herself to look directly at him. He smiled at her and her heart actually fluttered. The smile made him breathtakingly handsome.

'Do you work here every day?' he asked.

She shook her head. 'Wednesday to Sunday.'

'Not enough people here on Monday and Tuesday?'

'Those days are usually slow.'

He tilted his head, eyeing her curiously. 'Do you like this kind of chancy existence?'

She instantly bridled at this personal probe. It smacked of a much superior existence, which he had probably enjoyed all his life. 'Yes, I do. I don't have to answer to anyone,' she said pointedly.

'You prefer to be independent.'

She frowned at his persistence. 'Would you mind keeping still while I sketch?'

In short, shut up and stop disturbing me.

But he wasn't about to take direction from her. He probably didn't take direction from anyone.

'I don't want a still-life portrait,' he said, smiling the heart-fluttering smile again. 'Just capture what you can of me while we chat.'

Why did he want to chat?

He couldn't be attracted to her. It made no sense that a man like him would take an interest in a woman so obviously beneath his status.

Jenny forced herself to draw the outline of his head. Getting his hair right might help her with the more challenging task of capturing his face.

'Have you always wanted to be an artist?' he asked.

'It's the one thing I'm good at,' she answered, feeling herself tense up at being subjected to more curiosity.

'Do you do landscapes as well as portraits?'

'Some.'

'Do they sell?'

'Some.'

'Where might I buy one?'

'At Circular Quay on Mondays and Tuesdays.' She flashed him an ironic look. 'I'm a street vendor and it's tourist stuff—the harbour, the bridge, the opera house. I doubt you'd be interested in buying.'

'Why do you say that?'

'I think a *name* artist would be more your style.'

He didn't rise to the note of derision in her

voice, affably remarking, 'You might make a name for yourself one day.'

'And you want the pleasure of discovering me?' she mocked, not believing it for a moment and feeling more and more uneasy about why he was engaging in this banter with her.

'I'm here on a journey of discovery.'

The whimsical statement teased her into asking, 'Where are you from?'

'Italy.'

She studied his face; smooth olive skin, definitely a Roman nose, and that sensual mouth seemed to have Latin lover written all over it. His being Italian was not surprising. As she started sketching his features, she commented, 'If you wanted a taste of Venice, surely it would have been much easier to go there.'

'I know Venice very well. My mission is of a more personal nature.'

'You want to find yourself?' she tossed at him flippantly.

He laughed. It gave his striking face even more charismatic appeal. Jenny privately bet he was a devil with women and wished she could inject that appeal into his portrait, but the vibrant expression was gone before she could even begin to play with it on paper. The sparkle in his eyes gave way to a look of serious intent—a look that bored into her as though determined on penetrating any defensive layer she could put between them.

'I came for you, Isabella.'

His soft and certain use of her friend's name shocked her into staring at him. How could he know it? She signed her portraits *Bella,* not *Isabella.* Her mind reeled back over this whole strange encounter with him; the fact that he didn't fit her kind of clientele, his too-acute observation of her, his curiosity about her work, the personal questions. A sense of danger clanged along her nerves. Was she about to be unmasked as a fraud?

No!

He thought she was Bella. Which meant he hadn't known her friend. He must have got the name from one of the stall-holders who knew her as Isabella Rossini. Was he playing some supposedly seductive pick-up game with her? But why would he?

'I beg your pardon!' she said with as much indignation as she could muster, hating the idea of him digging for information about her, and thinking he could get some stupid advantage from it.

He gestured an apology. 'Forgive me for not being more direct in my approach. The estrangement in our family makes for a difficult meeting and I hoped to ease into it. My name is Dante Rossini. I'm one of your cousins and I'm here to invite you back to Italy for a reunion with all your other relatives.'

Jenny was totally stricken by this news. Bella had told her she had no family. There'd been no talk of any connections in Italy. But if there had been an estrangement, perhaps she'd never heard of them, believing herself truly orphaned by the plane crash which had killed her parents. On the other hand, was this man telling the truth? Even if he was, how would Bella have responded to it? No one from Italy had cared about her all these years. Why bother now?

Fear fed the burst of adrenaline that drove her to her feet. Fear chose the words that sprang off her tongue. 'Go away!'

That jerked him out of his air of relaxed confidence.

Jenny didn't wait for a response to her vehement command. She slammed down the stick of charcoal, ripped the half-done portrait off the easel, crumpled the sheet of paper up in her hands and threw it in the waste-bin to punctuate an emphatic end to this encounter.

'I don't know what you want but I want no part of it. Just go away!' she repeated, her eyes stabbing him with fierce rejection as he rose from the chair, suddenly taking on the appearance of a formidable antagonist.

'That I cannot do,' he stated quietly.

'Oh, yes you can!' Her mind wildly seized on reinforcements. 'If you don't I'll go to the forum management, tell them you're harassing me.'

He shook his head. 'They won't act against me, Isabella.'

'Yes, they will. They're very tight with security.'

He frowned at her. 'I thought you knew the Rossini family owns all the Venetian Forums. That you chose to buy one of our apartments here in Sydney because of the family connection.'

Her mind completely boggled. Had Bella known this? She had never mentioned it. And what did he mean…*all the Venetian Forums?* Was there a worldwide network of them? If so, the Rossini family had to be mega-wealthy and no one was going to take her side against this man. She was trapped on *his* territory.

'I've already spoken to the management here

about you,' he went on. 'If you need them to identify me, assure yourself that I am who I say I am, I'm happy to accompany you to the admin office…'

'No! I'm not accompanying you anywhere!' she almost shouted at him in panic.

Her raised voice attracted the attention of passers-by, including Luigi, the photographer, who dropped his hustling for clients to stroll over and ask, 'Having trouble here, Bella?'

She couldn't rope him in to help her, not against the man who had the management in his pocket. Luigi depended on his job here. The two men were eyeing each other over—both macho Italian males—and the bristling tension told her neither one of them was about to back down.

'It's okay, Luigi. Just a family fight,' she said quickly. He would understand that. Her experience of working in the forum had taught her that all Italian families got noisy over a dispute and were best left to themselves to sort out the problem.

'Well, tone it down,' he advised. 'You'll be scaring customers away.'

'Sorry,' she muttered.

He shrugged and moved off, tossing an airy wave at Dante. 'Make him take you to lunch. He looks as though he can afford it. A bit of vino…'

'Excellent idea!' her nemesis agreed. 'I'll help you pack up, Isabella.'

He turned and collected the folding chair he'd been sitting on before Jenny could say a word. She felt totally undermined by his arrogant confidence, helpless to fight the situation, yet desperate to escape it. He wasn't *family* to her, and what had seemed a harmless deception—a temporary lifeline that would help her and not hurt anyone—was turning into a murky mess that she didn't know how to negotiate.

'Why turn up now? Why?' she demanded of him as he carried the chair over to where she stood beside the easel.

'Circumstances change.' He flashed that smile

again. At close quarters it probably made every woman go weak at the knees and Jenny was no exception. Dante Rossini had megawatt sex appeal. 'Let me explain over lunch,' he added, his dark-chocolate eyes warm enough to melt resistance, his voice a persuasive purr.

Her spine tingled. Her heart pounded in her ears. Her mind screamed danger. No way could she give in to the charm of the man. If she didn't somehow extricate herself from this situation, it would lead to terrible trouble.

'You're too late,' she blurted out. It was the truth. Bella was dead. But she couldn't reveal that. 'I don't need you in my life. I don't want you,' she threw at him, wildly hoping he would accept that his mission was futile.

'Then why set yourself up in the Venetian Forum?' he shot at her, his eyes hardening with disbelief at her hysterical claims.

Bella had set her up. Confusion roared through Jenny. Had there been some artful plan behind her friend's kindness in inviting her to share the apartment, getting her employed here by using the Rossini name? Had Bella imagined it might catch the attention of the forum management enough to mention it to the Rossini family?

Was I bait?

Her first meeting with Bella…the offer that had seemed too good to be true…wanting to believe luck had smiled on her for once. Jenny shook her head. It was all irrelevant now. She shouldn't have stayed on, using Bella's name, getting herself in this awful tangle.

'Think what you like,' she snapped at the cousin who'd come too late. 'I'm out of here.'

She instantly busied herself, packing up the easel, her inner agitation making her hurry so much she fumbled and dropped the box of charcoal sticks. He swooped and picked it up, holding it out to her, making it impossible to completely ignore him. He was still holding her fold-up chair, as well.

'Thanks,' she muttered, snatching the box from him, stowing it in the carry-case.

'I'm not about to go away, Isabella,' he warned.

Her nerves quivered, sensing the relentless force of the man. With all that wealth and power behind him, he was undoubtedly used to people falling in with him. Being rebuffed and rejected would sting his ego, make him more persistent. It was imperative now to plan a disappearing act, get back to the apartment, pack only essentials, catch a bus, a train, a plane…anything that took *her* away. He wouldn't look for Jenny Kent. She was of no interest to him.

The carry-case was ready to go. She folded up the stool she used when sketching, tucked it under one arm, then steeled herself to face Dante Rossini and put an end to this danger-laden meeting. It took all her willpower to lift her gaze to his and hold it steady as she spoke to him, pouring a tone of flat finality into her voice.

'Don't waste any more of your time. Isabella

Rossini has not occupied any place in your family all these years and that isn't about to change because you suddenly want it to.' She held out her hand. 'Just give me the chair and let me go.'

He shook his head, unable to come to grips with her stance, not about to accept it, either.

Jenny panicked at the thought of having to endure more argument from him. 'Keep it then,' she cried, her hand jerking in a wave of dismissal as she turned away and forced her trembling legs to march across the forum, heading for the elevator that would shut him out and take her up to the apartment he couldn't enter.

The chair didn't matter.

It would have to be left behind anyway.

The only way to disappear was to travel lightly, go fast and far, leaving no trace for anyone to pick up.

CHAPTER FOUR

DANTE had never failed to deliver what his grandfather asked of him. Failure in this instance was unthinkable. He had to get Isabella Rossini to Capri.

He followed her determined walk away from him, staying a few steps behind, not attempting to catch up with her. He needed time to process her reaction, make some sense of it before tackling her unreasonable negativity again. He had anticipated a pleased response. The fact that she'd chosen to live and work at the Sydney forum after losing her parents had suggested a wish for contact with the family. He now had to get his head into gear to deal with something entirely different.

Angry pride?

A fierce independence, grown out of being left to fend for herself for so long?

There'd been fear in her eyes just before she'd turned her back on him. Fear of what? Change? The unknown?

Beautiful eyes. Even without any artful makeup they were stand-out eyes, their amber colour quite fascinating, shaded by long, thick curly lashes. He liked her wide, generous mouth, too, another stand-out feature in her rather angular face. Her hair was an unruly mop, but take her to a good stylist, get it shaped right, hand her over to a beautician to polish up the raw material, put her in some designer clothes—her figure was thin enough under that shapeless black gear to wear them well—and Lucia would be as jealous as sin over her newly discovered cousin.

And spitting chips over another grand-daughter to inherit some of Marco's estate.

The money…

He could use that as a bargaining tool. Isabella's parents had left her enough to buy the apartment but little more than that. She wouldn't have to work another day in her life if she pleased Marco. She could live like Lucia, being pampered in the lap of luxury. No woman in the world would knock that back. He just had to lay it on thickly enough for Isabella to take the bait.

Confidence renewed, Dante quickened his pace. She was heading into the passageway where the elevator to the south bank of apartments was housed. He glanced up, smiling at the colourful concoction the architect had designed—pink, lemon, green, red, blue, orange, purple—reminiscent of the brightly painted houses on the islands of Murano and Burano, a short ferry ride from Venice. Isabella's apartment was the purple one on the third floor. She had pots of pink geraniums on her balcony, a nice homely touch.

I don't need you in my life.

Dante's chest tightened as he remembered those vehement words. Maybe she didn't, but she could give up two months of it for Marco. Especially when the reward would be substantial. He'd pay her himself—upfront—if she doubted there was a pot of gold at the end of this trip. He'd spent thousands on Anya Michaelson to keep her sweet while he wanted her. He didn't care how much it cost him to give his grandfather the solace of making some peace with the past before he died.

Her finger jabbed the elevator button—an action of haste and anxiety. In her fast flight across the square, she hadn't once glanced back to check on what he was doing. Nor did she acknowledge his presence when he stood beside her, waiting for the elevator doors to open. She stared rigidly ahead as though he didn't exist.

Dante was not accustomed to being ignored. As much as he told himself not to be piqued by her behaviour—it would change soon enough with the lure of wealth—it took a considerable effort not to reveal any vexation when he spoke.

'I'm sorry I've upset you, Isabella. That wasn't my intention,' he assured her quietly.

No reply. Her jaw tightened. Dante imagined her clenching her teeth, denying the possible spilling of any more words to him. The stubborn stance irked him further. She was throwing out a challenge he'd take great satisfaction in winning, if only to see that rude rigidity wilt.

'I'd appreciate it if you'd listen to a proposition which is very much to your advantage,' he said, wondering if the blank wall she was holding was actually a negotiation tactic. Resistance virtually guaranteed being offered more.

The elevator doors opened. Her head jerked towards him. Her eyes slashed him with a cutthroat look. 'I'm *not* interested!'

Having punched out those decisive words, she stepped into the small compartment and hit the button for her floor.

Dante stepped in after her.

She glared at him, clearly seething with frustration. 'I told you…'

'I'm carrying your chair up for you,' he said blandly. 'You are rather loaded down with the rest of your working gear.'

She rolled her eyes away. The doors closed and she pointedly watched for the floor numbers to flash up, once again set on ignoring him. He noted that every line of her body was tense, fighting the pressure of his presence. She might be ignoring him but she was acutely aware of him.

A pity she was his cousin. He'd like nothing better than to have her at his mercy on a bed, begging him to do whatever he wanted with her. Now *that* would be very satisfying—seeing her stiff body quivering, surrendering to his will! But a bit too incestuous, given the close blood link. His grandfather wouldn't approve of that tactic.

The sexual scenario raised the possibility that

her love life might be a barrier. 'Is Luigi your boyfriend?'

The question startled her from her fixation on the upward journey of the elevator. 'No.' Worry carved a line between her brows. 'So don't pester him on my behalf. He's just a fellow worker. And don't go looking for other boyfriends, either, because there isn't one.'

'Good! No one to object to your coming to Italy with me.'

'Will you get it through your head I'm not going anywhere with you!' she cried in exasperation.

'Why not? There's nothing that can't be put on hold here. Why not satisfy a natural curiosity about the family you've never met?'

A frantic, cornered look in her eyes.

Was it a daunting prospect for her? Did she see herself being critically examined by a bunch of strangers?

'My grandfather...*your* grandfather...wants you with him, Isabella,' he pressed, then played his trump card. 'Marco is a very wealthy man. If you grant his wish, he will shower riches on you, give you access to more money than you've ever dreamed of. Financially your future—'

'I don't want his money!'

Horror on her face. Her whole body shuddered in recoil from the idea. Dante was so stunned by her reaction, he was totally at a loss to know what line of persuasion to try next. This woman was impossible. It was utter madness to be repulsed by the promise of financial security for the rest of her life.

The elevator came to a halt. She rushed out of it the moment the doors were open enough to make an exit, pelting along the corridor to her apartment as though the hounds of hell were snapping at her heels. Dante followed, grimly determined to get to the bottom of this crazy conundrum.

She shoved the key in the lock, was pushing against the door even before it opened. Dante knew she'd whirl inside and shut him out, given half a chance. He barged straight in after her before she could do it, not caring how outraged she'd be by the action. He'd run out of patience with trying to reason with her. If he had to tie her up and gag her, he would force her to listen to him long enough to be convinced that a trip to Capri was the best course for her to take.

'This is home invasion!' she yelled at him, her chest heaving in agitation. Nice breasts, Dante couldn't help noting.

'No reasonable person would think so. You didn't object to my carrying up the chair for you,' he calmly reminded her. 'Perfectly natural for me to step into your apartment with it.'

She dropped the carry-case containing her easel. The stool which had been tucked under her arm clattered to the floor. She reached out, grabbed the folded chair from him, and pointedly let it fall on top of the carry-case. Clenched hands planted themselves aggressively on her hips. Her eyes blazed rejection of any excuse he could give for entering her apartment without permission.

'Now get out!' she hurled at him.

'Not until I get satisfaction.'

He pushed the door shut and stood against it, blocking any move she might make to open it again. Dante wondered if she was going to fly at him and try to punch him out. Her eyes were wildly measuring his physique. Maybe she sensed that she'd stirred a dangerous male savagery in him, a savagery that would take pleasure in forcefully restraining any physical attack she made. His own hands were itching to demonstrate some mastery over her. She stepped back from the simmering flashpoint, lifted her chin to a defiant angle and spat out her next line of action.

'If you don't go right now, I'll call the police.'

'Go ahead. Call them,' he challenged without a flicker of care, confident of justifying his presence here.

She visibly dithered over the decision.

'While we're waiting for them to come, you can do me the courtesy of listening to why your grandfather wants you to visit him.'

She flinched at the mention of Marco, as though the idea of a grandfather wanting her was painful. Dante wished he knew what was going on in her head. He hated dealing blindly. But listening to him was a lot less bother for her than answering to the police, so he expected to win this round.

'Promise me you'll leave when you finish talking,' she demanded, hating him for forcing the choice.

He held up his hand. 'Word of honour.' He wasn't about to finish talking until she agreed to come with him.

She heaved a sigh, then with a much put-upon air, moved into the sitting room and settled herself in a bucket chair, hands folded in her lap, looking at him stony-faced. She reminded Dante of a rebellious student having to endure an unfair lecture from a headmaster before she could escape.

He propped himself on the well-padded armrest of a sofa, commanding the space between her and the door. 'What did your father tell you about the family rift?' he asked, wondering if his uncle Antonio had painted Marco in some false light to favour himself.

She shook her head. 'You talk. I'll listen.'

He talked, repeating his grandfather's story of what had led up to Antonio's banishment, filling in some facts about the rest of the family, the death of his own parents, Marco's grief at having lost two sons, the cancer that decreed he had only three months left to live—one month already gone—his search for Antonio which had led to Isabella, his wish to see her, get to know her.

He played on gaining her sympathy and was gratified when he saw tears well into her eyes. Sure that he could now clinch her co-operation, he finished with, 'He's dying, Isabella. The time is so short. If you can find it in your heart to give…'

'I can't!' she cried, covering her face with her hands as she sobbed, 'I'm sorry…sorry…'

'I'll organise everything, make it easy for you,' Dante pressed.

'No…no…you don't understand,' she choked out.

'No, I don't. Please tell me.'

She dragged her hands down her tear-streaked face, gulped in air, and raised a wet, bleak gaze to his. 'It's too late,' she cried in a grief-stricken voice. 'Bella died in a car accident six months ago. I thought she had no one. I didn't think it would matter if I took her identity for a while. I'm sorry…sorry that your grandfather thinks she's alive. Oh God!' she shook her head in wretched regret. 'I didn't mean to hurt anyone.'

Dante was totally floored. He'd been sent on an impossible mission. Another death. He closed his eyes, shutting out the imposter, thinking of his grandfather who'd been fooled into believing he had another Isabella who might look like his beloved wife. Everything within him railed against delivering such a devastating disappointment.

Anger stirred. Why hadn't the private investigators picked up the identity swap? How had this woman deceived everyone? No problem now in understanding her responses to him. She'd been scared out of her mind about getting tripped up. He opened his eyes to glare furious hostility at her.

'Explain to me how you managed to take Isabella's place without anyone questioning it,' he commanded, pushing himself upright and walking over to where she sat, standing over her, using deliberate intimidation to draw what he wanted out of her.

She didn't try to fight him this time. Her connection to his cousin poured from her in a stream of pleading for his understanding…how she'd come to share Isabella's apartment and use her name to get employment at the forum, the car accident, her friend burnt beyond recognition, her own identification cards destroyed in the fire, the mistake made by the authorities because of a handbag she'd been holding when she'd been thrown clear…

'I remembered afterwards that was why I'd taken off my seat belt. Bella was driving and she asked me to get a bag of sweets out of her handbag which she'd thrown onto the back seat. I couldn't reach with my seat belt on, so I unclipped it and leaned through the gap between the front seats, hooked my hand around the shoulder strap and dragged it onto my lap.'

'Her handbag must have contained her driver's licence,' Dante tersely pointed out. 'The identification photo…'

'It wasn't a good one of her. We both had long curly hair, hers darker, but that could have been from bad lighting when the camera shot was taken, and she was smiling so you couldn't tell her mouth wasn't as wide as mine. Her eyes were squinted up so their different shape wasn't so obvious, and I guess my face was bruised and puffy from the accident, making it look rounder. Even so, there was enough doubt about who I was for the police to call in the employment manager from the forum to identify me and because of my working under Bella's name...'

'Very convenient for you.'

She flushed at his acid sarcasm. 'I was in a coma for two weeks after the accident. The identification was made while I was still unconscious. I didn't know about it until after I woke up, and then all the medical staff was calling me Miss Rossini...and I let them. I let them because I had nowhere else to go and I needed recovery time from my other injuries, and I didn't think Bella would mind...'

'How could she?' Dante savagely mocked. 'She was dead.'

'Yes,' she agreed miserably. 'I'm sorry. I didn't know about you. Bella told me she was an orphan like me. No family. I didn't think it mattered when the police came again after I woke from the coma and I identified the driver as my flatmate, Jenny Kent...a nobody who wasn't connected to anyone. And that was the end of it.'

'Not the end. You took over Isabella's life because she had more than you,' he accused mercilessly. Money *was* a prime motivation. It always was. She'd just proved him right again.

'I only meant to do it for a while. Until I could...'

'Well, you fooled everyone effectively. You can go on fooling them for another two months.'

He would not fail his grandfather on what was virtually a death-bed request. It didn't matter who this woman was. She could make up for the deception she had played by being a good and loving grand-daughter to Marco until he died.

She shook her head, pained bewilderment in her eyes. 'I was going to leave here tonight, become Jenny Kent again. I'm sorry I...'

Ruthless purpose surged in Dante, cutting her

plan of escape dead. 'I will not allow you to destroy the hope that made my grandfather send me on this mission. You will come to Italy with me. You will stay with him in the villa on Capri until he no longer needs you. He will know you as Isabella…'

'No! No!' She leapt to her feet in panic, hands wildly gesturing protest. 'You can't! *I* can't!'

He gripped her flailing arms. His eyes burned through the glaze of horror in hers with unshakeable determination. 'I can and you will. If you don't do as I say, I'll call the police and have you arrested for identity-theft and fraud, and I promise you your term of imprisonment will be a lot longer than two months!'

Shock, fear, despair chased across her face.

'So what do you want to be, Jenny Kent?' he mocked. 'A common criminal rotting in jail or a pampered grand-daughter living in luxury?'

CHAPTER FIVE

Rome
One Week Later

JENNY stood in the bedroom assigned to her in Dante's palatial apartment and stared at her reflection in the mirror, barely recognising herself. She had been transformed into someone else— the Isabella Dante wanted to present to his grandfather. It was incredible what money could do; incredible, fascinating and frightening. It had the power to make anything possible.

She now had a passport in Isabella's name, an entire wardrobe of fabulous designer clothes— some acquired in Sydney while they waited for the passport, the rest bought during a stopover in Paris—a face that had been made over by a beautician, her once thickly tangled mass of hair cleverly cut into a tousled cascade of wild sexy curls, newly applied perfect fingernails, polished in a natural tone, plus a whole range of fantastic accessories to complement her new look—belts, bags, shoes, jewellery.

She'd flown halfway around the world in a private jet, been waited upon hand and foot, eaten food she'd never been able to afford, stayed in penthouse suites at the Gondola Hotels, and any minute now Dante would come and collect her for the helicopter flight to Capri. A different life, she thought. A totally different life which still didn't feel quite real to her.

This image in the mirror was Dante's puppet, moving and acting to his will. Even how it was dressed...

'Wear the Sass and Bide outfit,' he'd instructed. 'This first lunch at the villa will be informal, and the design is something fresh and individual. Lucia would not have seen it anywhere. She's not into Australian fashionistas.'

Lucia…Bella's other cousin.

Every time Dante mentioned her it was with a cynical twist. He didn't like her. Jenny had the strong impression he wanted his Isabella creation to outshine Marco's real granddaughter. Which felt terribly wrong to her, but maybe there was some good reason behind his antipathy towards his cousin. It was not her role to make judgements on the Rossini family. She had to follow Dante's edicts or… A convulsive shudder ran through her at the thought of imprisonment in a women's jail.

She couldn't face it. The rigid discipline of the orphanage still haunted her in nightmares. Being subjected to that kind of uncaring authority again—the unrelenting system of punishment for any infringement of the rules, fighting to survive with some sense of self intact—anything was better than suffering through another soul-destroying environment.

Somehow for the next two months she had to think herself into Bella's skin, be as true as she could to what her friend had told her about her life. If her presence helped Marco Rossini to die peacefully, maybe the deception wasn't such a bad thing. Whatever happened, this was Dante's choice, Dante's family, so he had to deal with the outcome. Though she was irrevocably tied to it.

No way out, she thought, hating the sense of being trapped, frightened of failing, frightened even more of never regaining her freedom. Two months…two months of a life she knew too little about. Would this incredible makeover Dante had orchestrated really help to blind the Rossini family to seeing she was not one of them?

The Sass and Bide outfit was startling, fascinating in its creative use of fabrics. The patchwork on the blue denim vest was quite wild with bits of lace, decorative buttons, braiding and embroidering. The short-sleeved white T-shirt underneath ended in jagged handkerchief points, just lapping over the matching blue denim hipster jeans which also had embroidery running down the legs, and buttons detailing the short side splits at her ankles.

She wore embroidered rope sandals on her feet, decorated with tiny lacy shells, and a matching rope handbag was slung over her shoulder. But that was where the trendy casual image ended. Dante apparently scorned costume jewellery. Sapphires went with blue denim; sapphire and diamond drop earrings and a gold chain watch with a sapphire face and diamonds marking the hours. In short, she was wearing a fortune, and the woman in the mirror could have stepped out of a magazine featuring incredibly wealthy celebrities.

'Ready?'

Her heart jerked. He even had a string on that,

Jenny thought as she swung around to face the all-powerful puppeteer. She'd left the bedroom door open for his manservant to collect her luggage which was all packed and ready to go. The man moved in behind Dante to do precisely that while his master—her master—strolled towards her, his gaze taking in her appearance from head to toe, making every nerve in her body twang with the need to be approved.

She took a deep breath, stiffened her spine and answered, 'As ready as I'll ever be.'

He smiled, apparently satisfied with how she looked, his dark eyes glittering with a sexy appreciation of the woman he'd fashioned to suit what he wanted. 'You look beautiful, Isabella,' he purred at her, and her whole body seemed to vibrate with self-awareness.

She'd never bothered much about her appearance. Clean and tidy was all she'd cared about, buying most of her clothes in charity shops, shying away from spending money on nonessentials because she might need it for living. Being dressed like this, being looked at as Dante was looking at her, evoked feelings she'd never felt before and she wasn't comfortable with them.

'I guess fine feathers make fine birds,' she muttered mockingly, thinking he always looked superb. He probably never glanced at a price-tag to see how much anything cost. He hadn't while shopping with her. No doubt the blue jeans and white sports shirt he wore carried designer labels. They certainly showed off his top-of-the-line physique—mega-male, oozing classy sex appeal.

'Don't duck your head,' he instructed, lifting a hand to her chin, tilting it up, forcing her gaze to meet his. 'Hold it high. You're proud to be Isabella Rossini. You've led an independent life and you won't kowtow to anyone. You're here because your grandfather invited you and that gives you every right to be treated as a respected member of the family, not Cinderella. Understand?'

It was difficult to find breath enough to speak when he was this suffocatingly close. 'Yes,' she choked out.

His thumb stroked her cheek. The hard ruthless gleam in his eyes softened to a wry appeal. 'I may not be allowed to stay at your side. If Nonno wants you to himself…be kind to him, Isabella. Put him at ease with you. I want him to be happy that you've come.'

Panic undermined the seductively soothing intent of his caress. Being left alone with Marco Rossini was a terrifying prospect. If Dante wasn't there to pull the strings…if she made a mistake…if she unwittingly revealed a different person to the one she had to portray…

Dante was frowning at her.

'I'll do my best,' she promised in a rush.

'There's nothing to fear,' he assured her, still frowning, his dark eyes stabbing his own in-domitable confidence into hers. 'I've paved the way for this meeting. Nonno will not be testing you about your identity. He's an old man, facing a painful death, wanting the pleasure of making your acquaintance. All you have to do is respond to him as warmly as you can.'

He made it sound easy. Maybe it was, though the deception still weighed on her mind. She scooped in a deep breath, trying to calm her jangling nerves, and lifted her chin away from his touch, needing to feel some independence. He had taken over her life to such an extent, it was difficult to be confident of standing alone, without his all-pervasive support.

'I'll do my best,' she repeated, and meant it, not wanting to be a source of distress to a dying man.

'It's in your best interests to do so,' he reminded her.

'Yours, too,' she said with a flash of resentment at the ruthless power he had wielded.

He smiled, amused by her counter-thrust at him. 'Yes. We're in this together, aren't we? You could say it forms an intimate bond.'

The hand he had dropped from her chin took possession of one of hers, fingers interlacing, gripping hard, enforcing a physical bond that burned like a branding iron, linking her inexorably to him. Jenny's heart fluttered wildly as the heat from his hand spread through her entire body, igniting a mad desire for an intimate relationship with Dante Rossini that was not based on deception.

'Time to go,' he said.

And Jenny went with him, once more a slave to his command, tugged along by his hand while her mind, which he couldn't completely dominate, was in a helpless whirl over the shocking realisation of finding herself actually *wanting* him to want her as a woman.

This situation was playing some weird sexual havoc on her. She'd been almost constantly in his company for a week, compelled into his world, and she supposed it was natural enough to have her normal, sensible self seduced by how beautiful and powerful and masterful he was—the kind of man that featured in foolish, romantic dreams, turning a Cinderella into a princess.

But this prince was not being driven by any desire for her.

She *knew* that.

He was determined on making his plan work, nothing more, nothing less.

It had to be these extraordinary circumstances causing her to be affected like this. They were thrown together by a conspiracy that probably bred a sense of closeness—a very temporary sense, she sternly reminded herself. When Dante no longer had any need for her co-operation, he'd cast her off as quickly and as ruthlessly as he'd picked her up.

To allow any attachment to him to develop was sheer stupidity. She had to keep remembering that Jenny Kent was not and would never be a person of serious interest to Dante Rossini. All he wanted of her was a brief impersonation of his cousin. If she played that role well enough, she'd be free to go at the end of it. That was what she had to aim for. Feeling swamped by this man's magnetic attraction could only create a problem for her and she had problems enough.

So don't go there.

Ever.

Dante was sharply aware of steel sliding into Jenny Kent's backbone as he walked her down to the car that would take them to the heliport. She held her head high, straightened her shoulders and adopted an aloof air, ignoring the fact that he was still holding her hand. He briefly wondered if the idea of having some blackmail power over him was inspiring the change. Or was she simply taking courage from his assurances?

For the most part, she'd given him passive obedience since he'd forced her to take on the role of Isabella. The only rebellion she'd staged was her refusal to talk about her own life, flatly telling him he didn't need to know. He wanted her to be Isabella and that was his only claim on her.

Oddly enough, it wasn't easy to shrug off his curiosity about Jenny Kent, probably because most of the women he met were only too eager to tell him about themselves, courting his interest, wanting him to know them. Of course, none of them had been an unwilling captive in his company, but he was willing to bet that a week of being pampered with luxury, beautified, outfitted with 'fine feathers' would normally thaw any resistance they might have to giving him whatever he wanted.

Not his manufactured cousin.

She didn't even speak unless spoken to. She soaked up what he told her about the Rossini family and offered nothing about herself. He wished there'd been time to have Jenny Kent investigated. He was taking a risk in trusting her to fulfil the role he'd insisted upon, trusting her fear of the alternative. His gut instinct told him she would deliver, which was all he should care about, yet it was definitely tantalising that she held herself so rigidly apart from any personal connection to him.

It gave him a perverse kind of pleasure to take possession of her hand. The urge to break her passivity kept niggling at him. But she didn't fight the contact, didn't respond to it in any way, just waited until he released it when she was stepping into the car, then sat with both her hands linked on her lap—a pointed picture of self-containment.

She did not so much as glance his way on the drive to the heliport, staring out the side window, apparently immersed in the sights and sounds of the streets they travelled. Dante felt himself challenged by her silence, by her stubborn determination to ignore him.

'What do you think of Rome?' he asked.

'It doesn't matter what I think,' she said dismissively, still not turning her head towards him.

'Nonno will ask. You might as well practice a reply.'

'Then I'd sound rehearsed. Better that I don't.'

'I've been rehearsing you all week. Why stop now?'

'Because time's up. I'm about to go on stage and stuffing any more into my head at this point will only make me more anxious about my performance.'

It was a fair argument so he let his frustration with her slide. Whoever Jenny Kent was, she was far from stupid. Not only did she have street smarts, but also quite an impressive natural intelligence, making his task of coaching her into meeting any expectation of Isabella a relatively easy one. Her life experience was obviously a far cry from his, yet he was confident she could now fit in to the family without feeling too much like a fish out of water.

In fact, she wouldn't just fit in, she'd shine. He'd been right about how she could look.

Nonno was going to be proud to own her as his grand-daughter. She *was* beautiful. Quite enticingly beautiful. But he couldn't afford to think of her like that. Nonno might see it in his eyes. Just one slip—revealing that she stirred a devilish desire in him—and the deception might unravel.

They arrived at the heliport. As Dante escorted his newly found cousin across the tarmac he watched his pilot's reaction to her. Pierro was standing by the opened door of the helicopter, waiting to greet them and help them to their seats. He'd seen Dante with many beautiful women in tow. 'Isabella' lit up his eyes with a look that said 'Wow! Knockout!' in no uncertain terms.

Pierro couldn't do enough for her, fussing over getting her comfortably settled in the helicopter. It won him a smile and sweetly appreciative words, neither of which had come Dante's way all week. It was absurd to feel a twinge of jealousy, but damn it! He'd done a hell of a lot for her and she was barely civil to him.

You've done it *to* her, not *for* her, he reminded himself, but he was still piqued that with him she wrapped herself in a cool dignity he couldn't penetrate. But he would. It was only a matter of time, and he'd make sure he had plenty of that with her while she was on Capri.

They landed at the villa just before noon.

Lucia, of course, was hot to meet her Australian cousin and size her up, actually coming down to the helipad instead of waiting in the shade of the colonnaded walkway. Dante felt the rush of adrenaline that always fired him up for critical meetings.

Game on! he thought, and hoped 'Isabella' was up to it.

'Your cousin, Lucia,' Dante murmured as he took Jenny's arm, holding her steady for the high step down from the helicopter.

Jenny had already mentally identified her. Due to the shopping experience with Dante in Paris, she instantly recognised French chic. Lucia Rossini personified it: short black hair artfully cut in an asymmetrical bob; a gorgeous scarlet-and-white dress that skimmed her slim, petite figure; elegant white sandals with intricate straps around her ankles. She also carried herself with the same arrogant confidence that Jenny now associated with great wealth.

Without Dante's intervention in dolling her up, she would have felt like dirt beneath the other woman's feet. The style he'd chosen for her was very different, but it had more than enough unique class to make Lucia look quite miffed as she eyed her newly arrived cousin. It made her wary as Dante moved her forward for introductions.

'Lucia, how sweet of you to welcome Isabella so eagerly!' he drawled, his lightly mocking tone putting Jenny even more on guard.

'Well, naturally I'm curious about a cousin I've never known, Dante,' she tossed back at him, a flash of venom in her dark eyes.

Certainly no love lost between these two, Jenny thought.

'*You've* had her to yourself for a whole week. Now it's my turn,' Lucia said, re-arranging her expression into a smile which didn't quite reach her eyes. 'Welcome to Capri, Isabella. I aim to make you feel at home here very quickly.'

She stepped forward, put her hands on Jenny's shoulders and air-kissed both cheeks. Jenny instinctively reared back, not used to people invading her personal space and not liking the over-familiarity, particularly since she felt no warmth coming from this cousin.

'Thank you,' she muttered. 'Very kind.'

'Isabella is Australian, Lucia,' Dante dryly reminded her. 'She's not accustomed to the Italian style of greeting. A hand-shake is more their style.'

'Oh! How stand-offish!' Lucia shrugged. 'I thought Australians were known for their open friendliness.'

Jenny flushed at the implied criticism. 'I'm sorry. I guess I'm feeling a bit strange at the moment. All this is very new to me.'

'Well, you'll have to learn to be Italian, too, if you want to fit into this family.'

The sheer arrogance of that statement stung Jenny's deep resentment at being forced into this situation. 'Maybe I won't want to fit in.' The words were out in a flash and she didn't regret them. In fact, it gave her a fine satisfaction to see Lucia's eyebrows shoot up in *unplanned* astonishment, as though being in the Rossini family was the most desirable thing in the world. It wasn't, as far as Jenny was concerned. 'I didn't ask to come here,' she added for good measure.

Lucia turned an arch look to Dante, her eyes glinting with malicious glee. 'This must be a first for you,' she drawled, 'running into resistance from a woman, not having her falling on her knees to please you. Nonno should have sent me to collect Isabella. I would have done a better job of it.'

'I doubt your brand of sly sniping would have achieved anything,' he replied sardonically. 'But then you wouldn't have wanted to, would you, Lucia? Isabella is too much a wild card for your liking, coming in at the death, so to speak.'

'Oh!' She feigned hurt shock. 'That's such a mean thing to say! Don't take any notice of him, Isabella.' A cajoling smile was directed at her. 'That's just a payback for being teased about his famous charm. I'm delighted that you're here for Nonno.' She waved an open invitation. 'Now do let's go up to the villa. It's so hot out here.'

Jenny glanced back at the helicopter, wishing she had never set foot in this place.

'Pierro will bring in our luggage,' Dante quickly assured her, taking her hand again, pressing it hard to remind her there was no escape, not until he allowed it, and that would be no time soon.

She hated him in that moment, hated having no choice, hated being thrust into such foreign territory, hostile territory if Lucia's attitude was anything to go by.

Capri was supposed to be a romantic place, a paradise for lovers. As they moved from the open heat to the shade of a colonnaded walkway, Jenny couldn't help thinking there was at least one serpent in this Eden.

How many more would she have to meet?

She was imprisoned on this island as surely as she would have been in a women's jail, having to work out how to deal with the other inmates and survive. The luxury of it was supposed to sweeten her term here, but wasn't there a saying—wealth is the root of all evil?

She yearned for her own simple life.

And hated Dante for forcing her into his.

CHAPTER SIX

THE colonnaded walkway was beautiful, shaded by pine trees and masses of brilliant bougainvillea. Jenny could imagine a Roman emperor with a string of courtiers strolling along it, sandals slapping on the flagstones. She wondered if Marco Rossini presided over his family like an emperor, parcelling out power to those who pleased him. Like Dante.

'I've had the blue suite in the guest wing made ready for you,' Lucia cooed at her. 'I'm sure you'll enjoy staying there. It has a lovely view of…'

'I don't think so,' Dante cut in with an air of haughty command. 'Isabella will feel much more comfortable in the suite adjoining mine.

Makes it easier for her to come to me if she has a problem. I did promise her my protection on this journey.'

It was the first Jenny had heard of his promised protection, but she didn't contradict him, thinking she might need it if Lucia was planning to sink her snaky fangs into her. Putting her in the guest wing, away from the puppeteer's support, was probably a ploy to make her more accessible to hostile action, as well as making her feel like an outsider, which she was, but she wasn't supposed to be.

'But Isabella is safely here,' Lucia argued. 'What possible problem could she have now?'

'Do as I say, Lucia.' No moving him on that point.

'It can't be done,' she said with a much put-upon sigh and a smug look at Dante. 'Anya Michaelson is already in the suite adjoining yours. Which is where *you* wanted her on previous visits.'

Dante's grip on Jenny's hand tightened, revealing a rise in tension. She glanced at his face.

Displeasure was written all over it. 'Anya came here uninvited?' he bit out in cold anger.

If Anya was his current girlfriend, she'd just made a bad move, Jenny thought. Dante Rossini liked to order things his way, and not even the lure of sexual pleasure right next door changed that aspect of his character.

'No, no. I invited her,' Lucia replied, still smug about her initiative. 'I flew over to Rome to do some shopping and ran into her on the Spanish Steps. She was most upset about your leaving so abruptly, without a word to her, so I explained about Nonno sending you off to fetch Isabella, and then I thought you'd like some relaxation with Anya after such an arduous trip....'

'In short, you interfered with what was none of your business.'

His tone would have made most people shrivel, but Lucia obviously thrived on his anger, positively enjoying herself.

'You should be more caring of your women,

Dante,' she trilled back at him. 'I was simply saving you from a nasty scene with Anya when you finally caught up with her again. I'm sure she'll now be ever so sweet to you, all primed to smooth away your travel fatigue.'

Jenny felt a strong distaste for this conversation. She looked at the pots of flowers spaced between the columns, pretending total disinterest in Dante's sex life, trying to keep herself emotionally separated from affairs that had nothing to do with her. Absolutely nothing.

Of course he would have a woman. What man like Dante Rossini wouldn't? And no doubt Anya was beautiful and very beddable. Despite his annoyance at Lucia's interference, Jenny expected him to choose the ready pleasures of a lover, especially since the arrangement was already in place. The potted flowers were lovely; geraniums, petunias, impatiens…

'Bad judgement, Lucia,' he said contemptuously. 'Family takes priority at a time like this.

You can deal with moving Anya out while I'm introducing Isabella to Nonno.'

A huge tide of relief swept through Jenny. His connection with her remained firm. *She* was more important to him than anything else. No, the *deception* was, she quickly corrected herself. He wasn't about to abandon her during this testing time, not when his grandfather's peace of mind was at stake. That came first. She kept her gaze trained on the flowers, but she heard real shock in Lucia's response.

'Don't be so unreasonable!' she snapped. 'It's not going to hurt Isabella…'

'This is not open to argument, Lucia. You chose to invite Anya. She's your responsibility. Do whatever you like with her, but Isabella is to occupy the suite next to mine. Make no mistake about that,' he said with steely authority.

'Anya won't like it!'

'Anya should have waited for me to contact her. *If* I wanted to.'

'How can you be so cruel! She loves you.'

'Since when have you become an authority on love?' he mocked.

'The two of you have been an item all this year.'

'Don't play games with me, Lucia. You'll lose. Every time.'

His tone had moved to studied boredom. Jenny had no doubt that for him the issue was closed. She could feel Lucia seething with frustration, but had no sympathy for her. To her mind, people who set out to make mischief should be caught in their own net and made to pay.

'One day your insufferable ego will be your undoing, Dante,' Lucia warned venomously.

A little shiver of apprehension ran down Jenny's spine. It was probably Dante's ego that refused to accept failure, forcing her into this false identity. If Lucia somehow uncovered the deception…

'Don't hold your breath waiting for that day, Lucia,' he drawled, emitting a confidence that eased Jenny's spurt of fear, though didn't completely eliminate it. Two months was a long time to be under the gun from *this* 'cousin.'

'Anyway, I can't deal with Anya now. Nonno is waiting for us on the terrace.'

'He's not waiting for you,' Dante coldly corrected her.

'I won't be shut out of Nonno's first meeting with Isabella. He expects us to be all together.'

'I'll tell him you've already met Isabella. I doubt you'll be missed. Nonno will want to focus all his attention on the grand-daughter he doesn't know yet.'

'It's a point of hospitality, Dante,' she grated out angrily.

'If you insist on accompanying us, I'll let him know just how inhospitable you've been, putting *your* guest ahead of the very special family member Nonno wants to feel welcomed here.'

'There's nothing wrong with the Blue Suite! Isabella, I promise you it's beautiful.'

Jenny didn't want to be dragged into the argument, but the direct appeal to her couldn't be ignored. The colonnaded walkway had led into a fantastic atrium where they had come to a halt while the conflict was settled. It had a central water feature—a pool covered with gorgeous water-lilies—and she reluctantly lifted her gaze from these to look at Lucia.

Her younger 'cousin's' dark eyes burned with the demand that she fall in with her plan, woman to woman against the man who divided them. For a moment Jenny was almost tempted, just to rattle Dante's overbearing power, but the situation was too tricky for her to negotiate alone.

'I'm sorry you're being put to so much trouble on my account, Lucia,' she said as calmly as she could, trying to maintain a composure that hid a growing mountain of nervous tension. 'It *is* difficult, being a stranger to all this.' She gestured to the exotic surroundings. 'Dante has shepherded me around all week. Having him close by will make it easier for me.'

The hand holding hers squeezed approval, making her feel too connected to him again, too aware of him in a way that would not lead to anything good for her. He was her captor, her jailor, and while he probably meant to give her a sense of safety, he kept shaking her up with an attraction she knew was treacherous. Having him in the suite next to hers was not going to make life here easier for her, yet being separated from him was too scary to contemplate.

'A fine start, Lucia,' Dante mocked. 'You've had Isabella apologising twice to you in the past ten minutes, making her feel uncomfortable.'

'I didn't mean to,' she flared at him, furious at being out-manoeuvred.

'Then you can demonstrate a kinder nature by making instant amends.' He waved her towards one of the wide hallways which ran off from the atrium. 'I'll make your excuses to Nonno.'

Her jaw clenched. Every atom of her being exuded hatred of defeat, the knowledge that she was forced to accept it. *This time around.* Dante had her cornered with no way out. He was very good at that, Jenny thought with black irony.

Lucia managed to stretch her mouth into a smile aimed at her. 'I truly had no intention of making you feel uncomfortable, Isabella. Please forgive my thoughtlessness.'

'I don't mean to be difficult, either,' she replied with an answering smile. 'I guess I haven't yet recovered from the shock of being presented with a family I knew nothing about. I can understand it's a shock to you, as well.'

Lucia seized the excuse. 'Yes. Hard to know what to do for the best. I'll go and fix everything up for you and join you on the terrace as soon as I can.' With a last challenging glare at Dante, she turned on her heel and walked briskly to the hallway he'd indicated.

'Well done,' Dante murmured, his warm breath

wafting over Jenny's ear, making her flinch away from the tingling sensation.

Her head jerked up, her eyes rejecting any form of intimacy with him as they met and held his. 'Bella might very well have walked away after one day of this rotten family rivalry,' she said in a fierce whisper. 'Why don't I do that, Dante? Remove any danger of being caught out. You got me here, which is all your grandfather asked you to do. Be satisfied with…'

'No!' He cut her off, ruthless determination stamping on her rebellion. 'I've paid for the performance. You give it.'

'One day is enough,' she argued on a wave of panic.

'It won't be for Nonno.' He released her hand and took hold of her upper arms, forcing her to face him. His dark eyes blazed with relentless purpose. 'While ever he lives, you stay here, giving him whatever he wants of you.'

She instinctively fought against the overwhelming pressure of his demands, frantically searching for some way out. 'What if he doesn't like me?'

'He will.'

'Why should he? He doesn't know me.'

'Neither do I but I like you, Isabella.' The tension on his strong face broke into a slow, sensual smile. 'I'm beginning to like you very much.'

Her heart skittered in wild alarm as she felt her resistance melting. Her mind screamed that he had a woman and she must not allow his famous 'charm' to get to her. 'I haven't given you any reason to,' she snapped.

He laughed, effectively zooming up his attraction quotient which was already far too discomforting for Jenny. Her head whirled with the need to block it out, stay indifferent to him.

'All this time we've spent together, not once have you whined or wailed or wept about your fate.'

'There was no point in kicking and screaming over what I can't change.'

'Exactly. Which is a surprisingly intelligent response from a woman.'

'Then you can't know many intelligent women.'

'Or you're not practised in using feminine wiles to win what you want.'

He was right. She'd never learnt to use feminine wiles, never been in the kind of environment where they might have been of use. In any event, if she read his character correctly, they would have been futile weapons in this situation.

'Would they have worked on you?' she asked, showing her scepticism.

'No. But that wouldn't have stopped most women from using them.'

'Waste of time and energy,' she muttered.

'True. And I appreciate your pragmatic attitude. Needs must to get the job done. You've actually given me many reasons to like you, Isabella. Not least of which was the deft way you handled Lucia.'

'As you said, you've paid for the performance. I was simply following your lead.'

'With a nice little embellishment of your own at the end.' He smiled again as he lifted a hand to touch her cheek in an admiring salute. 'I'm sure you'll handle the meeting with Nonno just as well.'

Her skin burned under the light caress. Her eyes burned with resentment over the cavalier way he touched her as he liked, always reinforcing the inescapable link between them. An increasingly dangerous link in Jenny's mind.

'Let's get on with it,' she said tersely.

'It will go better if you relax.'

'I'll relax more quickly if you get your hands off me.'

He raised his eyebrows at the too-revealing comment and Jenny cursed herself for letting it slip. He lifted his hands out in a gesture of meaning no offence, and she felt herself flushing as she rushed into answering the heart-pumping speculation in his eyes.

'You might own me in one sense, Dante Rossini, but there are some liberties you have no right to take.'

He nodded but the speculation didn't go away and she inwardly squirmed under it, knowing she had just shown a vulnerability that completely undermined any pose of indifference.

'Another first,' he murmured in dry amusement. 'No woman has ever objected to my touch before.'

'I'm your cousin,' she fiercely reminded him. 'And don't you forget it.'

'Cousins can and do show physical affection.'

'I can do without Lucia's brand of affection. And yours.'

He cocked his head musingly. 'Nonno will like your feisty sense of independence. I think you're ready to meet him now.'

'Do I have a choice?'

'No.'

'I didn't think so.' She waved a careless hand,

doing her utmost to appear relaxed. 'Lead on. I'm as ready as I'll ever be.'

Out of the corner of her eye she could see him smiling as he ushered her over to a set of double glass doors which opened to a terrace overlooking the sea they had flown over only a short while ago. The old saying—'caught between the devil and the deep blue sea'—slid into her mind. It was precisely how she felt.

Focus on what Bella would be feeling, she swiftly told herself. Here she was, meeting her grandfather for the first time, a man who'd wanted nothing to do with her family until now. Any sense of affection was impossible. Curiosity, yes. Perhaps resentment, too, at being called in so late in the day, too late for her own father who'd died in exile, never knowing any forgiveness for his grave teenage sin.

She mentally blocked out Dante, training her gaze on the old man being helped up from a sun-lounge by a woman caregiver. He still had a full head of thick wavy hair, shockingly snow-white, framing a face that seemed all bones, the flesh obviously wasted by the cancer that was eating him from the inside. His skin was tanned from lying in the sun, possibly in an attempt to look healthier than he was. He wore a loose white tunic over baggy white trousers. Neither hid the frailty of a body which had probably once been as big and strong as Dante's.

He was a dying man, maybe in considerable pain, warranting some sympathy despite the other circumstances that had brought her here. It was clearly an effort for him to stand straight and tall, determined on meeting her with dignity. Pride doesn't die, Jenny thought, and Bella might well be prickly with pride, too, the outcast who hadn't asked to be rejoined to this Rossini family and had no reason to bow to this patriarch.

Hold your head high, Dante had instructed.
She did.

And met Marco Rossini's penetrating dark gaze with determined steadiness.

I am Bella. You are my grandfather and you don't know me. This is not just a test for me. It's a test for you, too.

CHAPTER SEVEN

THEY stood, face-to-face, studying each other in a silence that stretched Jenny's nerves so far she could feel them twanging with tension. Marco Rossini was taking in every feature of her face as though trying to match them against some picture in his mind, and fear squeezed her heart as she read disappointment in them. Inevitable, she knew, because she had no Rossini genes, though maybe his disappointment was good for her. He mightn't want to keep her here, since she didn't look like the son he had banished.

His mouth finally broke into a wry little smile. 'Thank you for coming,' he said, his voice furred with emotion.

'I'm sorry it was too late for…for my father.' She hated speaking the deception that had to be carried through, but the sentiment was right if she'd been Bella.

'So am I, my dear. So am I,' he repeated sadly.

And her heart went out to him. It *was* sad, sadder than he knew with his grand-daughter gone, too. Tears welled into her eyes, remembering Bella's dreadful death, and Marco Rossini reached out and took one of her hands in both of his, patting it comfortingly.

'Your loss is even more grievous with both parents gone,' he said in gentle sympathy. 'I hope I can make up in some way for not being there for you.'

The tears overflowed, spilling down her cheeks. It was awful, pretending to be someone she wasn't. This should be happening to Bella, getting a grandfather who would care for her. She shook her head, bit her lip, swallowed hard, desperate to regain some control. 'I'm sorry,' she choked out. 'I didn't mean to…'

'It's okay, Isabella,' Dante soothed, quickly stepping over to a small table beside the sun-lounge, pulling some tissues out of a box and thrusting them into her hand. 'I'm sure Nonno understands this meeting isn't easy for you.'

'Come and sit down, my dear,' the old man invited, drawing her over to a bigger table shaded by a large umbrella. 'Pour her a drink, Dante.'

The table was round, the chairs well-cushioned. Marco dismissed his caregiver as Dante poured the three of them drinks from a jug of fruit-juice, adding ice from a more expensive version of an esky. The men sat on either side of her and Jenny did her best to regain some com-posure, mopping her cheeks, hoping the eye-makeup she'd been taught to apply wasn't completely messed up, taking several deep breaths to ease the tightness in her chest.

'Where is Lucia?' Marco asked his grandson, diverting attention from her while she recovered from her distress.

'Re-arranging accommodation for Isabella. She had designated the furthermost suite in the guest wing for her, which I didn't consider appropriate.'

'Ah! So typical!' the old man remarked ruefully. 'I should have directed the choice.'

'Lucia is used to being your only grand-daughter, Nonno.' He nodded towards Jenny, a silent warning that his cousin could be spiteful towards her.

'I'll take that into account. But for the most part, you'll have to be my watchdog, my boy.' It was a reluctant admission of weakness.

'I will,' Dante assured him.

'Put all business on hold. I want you here now. It won't be for long.'

'I've already done that, Nonno. I want to spend this time with you.'

The old man heaved a weary sigh. 'I don't have much energy these days. Thank you for bringing Isabella to me, Dante. She should not have been left alone.'

'I'll see that she is never without family support again.'

Jenny couldn't let that pass. 'I'm all right. I don't need anything from you,' she declared, shooting a frown at both Dante and Marco. 'I didn't come to get your family support. I can look after myself.'

The old man eyed her quizzically. 'Why did you come, Isabella?'

'Because…' *He forced me to,* but she couldn't say that. 'Because I wanted to know where my father had come from. Dante told me why you banished him, but you know, it must have been terrible for him, too, knowing he caused his mother's death. I think now he punished himself, taking on the hardships of living and working in the Outback. It's a very isolated life. But he was a good man, a good husband, a good father. You could have been proud of what he made of himself.'

She barely knew where the words came from— stories Bella had told about her growing-up years on the cattle station in far west Queensland, her own instinctive spin on the tragedy that had led to Antonio Rossini's exile, a need to resolve the bad feelings that Dante wanted resolved because that would free her in the end.

Her earnest outburst seemed to drive Marco back inside himself. He closed his eyes. His face sagged. His skin took on a greyish tinge.

Dante leaned forward, anxiously touching his arm. 'Nonno, Isabella didn't mean to be accusing.'

The heavy lids slowly lifted. 'My boy, I've been saying the very same things to myself, ever since I read the investigator's report.' He turned deeply regretful eyes to Jenny. 'What was done was done in anger and grief. I loved my wife very much. And I believe what you tell me. Antonio loved his mother very much. He gave you her name.'

Dante hadn't mentioned that to her. It made more poignant sense of Marco's disappointment. 'You wanted to see her in me.'

'Yes. Antonio looked very like her. I thought…' He made an apologetic grimace.

'It's Isabella on my birth certificate but I've always been called Bella,' Jenny said defensively, shying from being linked to the woman whom Marco had loved and lost. It made her feel even more of a fraud.

'Bella…' he repeated softly. 'A fitting name. You're a beautiful young woman. Your mother must have been beautiful, too.'

Jenny flushed at the compliment, knowing it wasn't really deserved since her 'beauty' had been engineered by Dante. 'I thought so,' she answered stiffly, judging it to be the safest reply.

'Do you have photographs of your parents you can show me?'

Jenny shook her head, answering with Bella's own words explaining why she had none of the usual mementoes of her family. 'The old homestead on the station burnt down when I was eighteen and in my last year at boarding school.

My parents were away at the cattle sales. Nothing was saved.'

'Another loss for you,' Marco murmured sympathetically.

'And you.' Her eyes flashed understanding of his desire to see a pictorial record of the son who had lived out his life on the other side of the world.

'Yes. But I chose to bring my loss upon myself. You didn't.'

It was fair comment and she nodded her appreciation of it. She was beginning to like Marco Rossini. He didn't come over as a cruel tyrant, ruthlessly wielding his wealth and power to punish or reward, more a man in the winter of his life, regretting mistakes he could not re-write.

She picked up the drink Dante had poured for her and sipped the fruit-juice, grateful for the cool moisture sliding down her throat. It tasted of pineapple and oranges. She needed the refreshment for the next round of questions.

A glance at Dante showed him watching her with an air of curious respect, as though she'd met more than his expectation in her performance so far. Which was a huge relief, since she'd been winging it with a mish-mash of her own feelings and what she'd imagined Bella's would be.

'Since you chose to live at the Venetian Forum, I thought Antonio must have told you some of his family history,' Marco put to her. 'Yet you said you knew nothing of us.'

'He never spoke of you,' she answered, though she had no idea of whether that was true or not. The question of why Bella had bought an apartment at the Venetian Forum had been tormenting her ever since Dante had brought it up. She had to produce a logical reason for it.

'We had an Italian name. I asked my father where it had come from. He told me it was an old Venetian name. His family had lived there but when he'd lost them he'd emigrated to Australia, and Venice was a place in the past for him. He said I should only think about being an Australian.' She lifted her chin proudly. 'Which is what I am.'

The old man nodded. 'It's a fine country. I spent some time in Sydney, purchasing suitable property for our hotel and the forum. It's a beautiful city.'

'Yes. I love it,' Jenny said strongly, wanting him to know she had no desire to leave her life for anything he could offer. Bella might have made that change but Jenny Kent couldn't.

'A big change for you from life in The Outback,' he remarked, possibly thinking if she could adapt to that, she could adapt to moving to another country.

'I had no heart for trying to run the cattle station after my parents died. There was a large mortgage on it because of the drought and…'

'Too difficult for you in every respect,' Marco murmured sympathetically.

'Yes.' She sighed over the immediate difficulty of trying to relive Bella's life. 'After everything was settled up, I wasn't sure what I wanted to do, so I went on what you might call a journey of discovery, travelling around until I found a place that appealed to me. When I came to Sydney, I found the Venetian Forum and…'

'And you remembered your father was originally from Venice,' Marco supplied helpfully.

'It felt right. Like a sense of belonging. I loved the artiness of it, the colours of the apartments, the markets around the canal. I've always loved drawing and I thought about signing up for an art course but I had to wait until the beginning of the new year to do that. I made a good friend who was also into art and asked her to share my apartment so I wasn't alone. She didn't have any family, either. We were like sisters.'

Jenny desperately hoped that covered everything. 'But then I lost her, too,' she finished off, her voice losing traction under the dampening weight of sorrow that Bella's death always evoked in her.

She closed her eyes and ducked her head, fighting another rush of tears. Bella should be here, not her. Jenny Kent had no one to care if she was dead or not. And Bella had been so kind to her, so generous in her sharing, so good to be with. She had deserved more from life, and maybe she had secretly yearned for this reunion with the Rossini family.

Jenny wept for her in her mind…. *I can't do this for you. I'm not you.* Yet to survive she had to take Bella's place for Marco Rossini. Dante would not let her go until the performance was no longer needed for his grandfather.

'You have us now, Bella,' the old man assured her quietly.

She shook her head and lifted a bleak gaze to the man she had to satisfy. 'You don't feel real to me, Mr Rossini. None of this feels real. I'm apart from it.' That was the truth.

'Give it time, my dear. I know about the accident that killed your friend. You've suffered one tragedy after another and it's taken a good part of this year for you to recover from your own injuries, delaying the career plan you'd decided upon. Let this visit to Capri be a healing time for you, in many respects. We'll get to know each other…'

Panic churned through her again at the thought of keeping up this deception every day for months. She couldn't do it, couldn't… 'But you're going to die, too,' she blurted out, wildly hoping he would understand she couldn't bear it. 'Dante wouldn't take no for an answer, so I came to see you, but…'

There was an instant hiss of indrawn breath from Dante, a tense leaning forward.

Jenny was too scared to look at him, too scared to utter another word. Her eyes frantically pleaded with his grandfather to let her off the hook.

The old man raised a commanding hand to his grandson. 'There's no need to be protective of me, Dante. Why should Bella risk growing fond of a man she knows is dying?'

'You're her grandfather,' he answered vehemently.

Jenny trembled at the sound of his displeasure.

'Who has never played any part in her life, never done anything for her,' Marco replied reasonably. With an air of sympathetic understanding, he turned to Jenny, addressing her kindly. 'My dear, I have no doubt Dante did everything in his power to steam-roll you into this visit. I'm sure he would have played upon your natural urge to see where your father came from.'

She flushed, ashamed of the lie.

'Antonio was my son for eighteen years,' he went on in a tone of sad yearning. 'He was a boy of great promise. One thing I can do is fill in those years for you, if you'll allow me.'

Her heart sank. Bella would have wanted that.
Any daughter who'd loved her father would. She
could feel Dante fiercely willing her to agree,
hanging the threat of prison over her head if she
didn't. There was no way out.

'I have very little time left, Bella,' Marco added
softly. 'Will you help me to spend it well, cor-
recting a wrong that weighs heavily on my
heart? Think of me, if you will, as a treasure
chest of memories you can open now, but will
be forever closed once I'm gone.'

It was too persuasive an appeal to deny. 'All
right. I'll try it,' she conceded, surrendering to the inevitable once again. 'I'm sorry. I
shouldn't have thrown your…your failing health
in your face. It just seems that…'

'Death keeps cutting through your life?'

She nodded, feeling too uncomfortable to say
anything more.

'It's different with me, Bella. My journey is
simply drawing to a close. Only this business

with you remains undone.' He smiled encourage-ment at her. 'Let's finish it together.'

She managed a wobbly smile back. 'I hope it will be good for you, Mr Rossini.'

'Good for you, too, my dear.'

Not in a million years, Jenny thought darkly.

She threw a defiant look at Dante, not really caring about his reaction to her performance since Marco was satisfied with the end result. Besides, she was too drained of feeling by this traumatic meeting to worry about him at this point.

'It will be all right, Isabella. I promise you,' he said quickly, determined on soothing her fears.

He'd stand between her and any trouble. Jenny had no doubt about that. But he couldn't promise it would be all right for her. It never could be. The deception was tearing her apart. The bitter irony was she had thought surviving a term in a women's prison would be harder.

Bad choice.

Bad, bad choice.

Jenny Kent was more in danger of losing herself here than anywhere else.

CHAPTER EIGHT

'You like living dangerously?'

The angry threat in Dante's voice was like a hammer beating on Jenny's head, which was already aching from the stress of the meeting on the terrace. Lucia had joined them there. Lucia had shown her to this suite so her new cousin could freshen up before lunch. Dante, of course, had tagged along to ensure everything was 'all right,' and once they had entered the appointed room, he'd very purposefully ushered Lucia out, closing the door firmly behind her, intent on securing a private tête-à-tête with the puppet who'd done her own little dance with his grandfather.

Jenny gritted her teeth and turned to face him,

determined on standing the ground she had just established with Marco Rossini—an independent person who'd make her own choices. Trapped here she might be, but she wasn't going to bend to Dante's will anymore. She met his blazing gaze with stubborn defiance.

'I adapted to circumstances. Isn't that what you wanted of me?'

'You saw a chance to extract yourself from the situation and you took it,' he fired at her.

'I'm not what he wanted,' she retorted fiercely. 'I couldn't be, could I? You should have foreseen that, Dante. You disappointed him.'

'No. I have never disappointed my grandfather,' he declared with vehement conviction. 'One of his wishes didn't come true. You don't look like Antonio. That was unavoidable, but you can and will supply everything else he needs from you.'

'I said I'd try.'

He crossed the room to where she stood at the foot of the bed, towering over her with intimidating power. 'You were *trying* to twist your way out of this. Don't *try* it again or I'll make you pay for it.' His eyes bored into hers. 'Believe me, I'll make you pay for it.'

She believed him.

He was as much tied to this deception as she was, and failure was unacceptable.

Dante Rossini didn't fail.

The force of the man in such close proximity made her quake inside. It was like being blasted by an electric energy that jangled her nerves, kicked her heart into a faster beat, tore at her muscles, leaving them quivering. She stared back at him, refusing to let him see any weakness in her, silently fighting her lonely fight to survive him as well as everything else.

'Nothing more to say?' he mocked.

She swallowed convulsively, trying to get some control over her throat muscles. Her mouth was as dry as the Sahara Desert, making it impossible to speak, so she simply shook her head.

He didn't want to hear anything she might say, anyway.

The threatening tension on his face slowly relaxed. The laser-like heat in his eyes simmered down. His mouth actually quirked into an ironic little smile.

'On the whole, you did quite well out there. Not the warm response I told you to give, but the emotional tears were good. Nonno was moved by them. He liked your independent stance, too.'

The approval, coming straight on the heels of his attack, turned Jenny's mind to mush.

'Just don't hold that line too hard,' he went on. 'You've made your point. You're not about to suck up to a grandfather who hasn't been a grandfather to you. That's okay. It's an attitude he respects, but soften it with kindness. And courtesy.'

She nodded.

He huffed an exasperated sigh. His eyes snapped with annoyance. 'We're back to the silent treatment, are we?'

It goaded her into a challenging glare and re-activated her vocal chords. 'Less grief for me if I remain a submissive doll who doesn't buck your authority.'

'Huh!' he scoffed. 'Submissive is the last word I'd apply to you! I'm not fool enough to believe something meek and mild resides in the fortress you've built around yourself. You can fly the white flag as much as you like but I know…'

He stepped closer, raising her tension level to screaming point. His hand gripped her chin, fingers pressing into the curve of her cheek, and his eyes were glittering with heat again, not angry heat, not threatening heat, more a very male sexual heat wanting supremacy over a woman. He was touching her, touching her aggressively, and she was paralysed with panic.

'I know rebellion is seething behind it,' he said with arrogant certainty. 'And maybe the best way to quell it is to storm your defences and seduce you into wanting to stick with me.'

His fingers slid into her hair. His other arm scooped her body hard against his. She had no time to react with any physical or vocal protest. His mouth covered hers, and the shock of his kiss, of being enveloped by the heat and strength of his powerful body, completely robbed her of any resistance. He invaded her mind, possessed it with a host of sensations.

She'd never been kissed like this before, never been held by a man like him, never experienced such an explosion of excitement. His mouth ravished hers, his tongue sweeping over her palate, making it tingle with intense pleasure, driving her own tongue into a duelling response. He had read her character rightly. Submission was not in her nature. Every primitive instinct she had was suddenly triggered, dictating a need to fight back, to do to him what he was doing to her.

The self-discipline that had ruled her life for so long broke into an angry passion. He held her body by force. She flung her arms around his head, hands burrowing fiercely into his thick hair, holding him just as forcefully. Her lower body ground against his. Her breasts thrashed his chest. No control. Every action was driven by a wild urge to assert herself, not surrender to his dominance, make him feel what he was making her feel.

The arm around her back tightened, his hand pressing down, grasping the fleshy curve of her bottom, lifting her into intimate contact with the erection she had aroused. Part of her mind registered danger. The rest of it revelled in her power to seduce him out of his formidable control.

He'd taken her out of the life she knew. She wanted him to pay for that, screw up his puppet plan, storm him with crashing waves of feeling, drag the devil into the deep blue sea he'd plunged her into. Awash with incoherent emotion, she was barely aware of him moving, carrying her with him. His mouth was locked on hers, kissing with ravaging intensity. Only when he'd tumbled her backwards onto the bed, did it break away.

Her eyes snapped open. He was kneeling over her, breathing hard, a dark confusion on his face. Words flew off her tongue in a silky taunt. 'Not what you wanted, Dante?'

His eyes blazed with the desire to crush her spirit, grind it so far down she'd be enslaved to his will. *Never,* she silently shot at him, exhilarated by the contest between them.

A knock on the door startled them out of the intense connection with each other. Dante cursed under his breath, backed off the bed, hauled her to her feet. 'This will keep,' he muttered savagely, releasing her to head for the door, putting respectable distance between them.

Jenny's legs were too tremulous to walk anywhere. She sucked in air to get a blast of oxygen through her scattered brain and sat back down on the bed, needing recovery time and wanting to hide any crumpling of the duvet where she had lain on it. Her heart was pumping with horror at what she had almost done with Dante Rossini, horror at her own mad elation over it.

They were supposed to be cousins. She bit down on a bubble of hysterical laughter. If this deception fell apart it would be his fault. He'd started it. He'd forced it. And be damned if she'd take the blame for it!

Another knock on the door.

He opened it. 'Anya?' he said in a tone so cold, it automatically denied there'd been any boiling heat in this room.

Anya…the woman he usually housed in this suite for his sexual convenience…here to smooth away his travel fatigue.

The hysterical laughter bubbled up again and Jenny clamped down on it, pride insisting on an appearance of absolute decorum. She sat up straight, hands in her lap, her mind seething with curiosity over how Dante was going to handle *this* deception, dealing with his current girlfriend after he'd just been conducting a sexual assault on *his cousin*. Was he incredibly adept at switching himself on and off?

She was curious, too, about the type of woman who usually attracted him. No doubt someone as fabulous as him in the looks department, she thought cynically, determined not to feel in any way jealous. This was not her world and she wasn't about to forget that reality.

'Excuse me, Dante,' Anya pleaded in a honeyed voice. 'Some of my toiletries were left in the bathroom. I've come to collect them.'

She didn't give him the chance to deny her entry, sliding into the room as she spoke, obviously keen to get a look at the cousin for whom she had been evicted from this suite. Anya Michaelson was a honey all over. Men probably flocked to her like bees. She had a glorious mass of silky blonde hair. Her figure was sensational, voluptuous curves barely encased in a bright yellow mini-dress. Perfect long legs gleamed as though they'd just been rubbed with scented oil. And the face she turned to Jenny was strikingly beautiful: flawless skin, stunning blue eyes, a full-lipped mouth with a very sexy pout.

'Sorry to break in on you like this,' she directed at Jenny, the blue eyes gobbling up every detail of her appearance, sharply assessing the attraction of the woman Dante was supposedly protecting. 'I'll only be a minute.'

She was already crossing the room, heading for a door which had to lead to an ensuite bathroom.

'Say hello to Isabella, Anya.'

The whip-like command from Dante stopped her in her tracks. 'Oh!' she exclaimed apologetically. 'I didn't mean to be rude.' A row of perfect white teeth was flashed at Jenny. 'Hello, Isabella. Don't you love Capri?'

'Not particularly,' Jenny answered, bridling at the condescending tone.

'Well, you've just arrived. I'm sure it will grow

on you. Excuse me while I remove my things, won't you? I expect we'll be meeting properly over lunch.' She threw an appeasing smile at Dante. 'Pardon me, *caro*. A careless oversight by one of the servants, not being thorough in checking what might have been missed.'

'Make sure you collect everything, Anya. I don't want you returning,' he said balefully.

She kissed her fingertips and tossed it at him, sashayed into the bathroom, leaving the door open behind her, not so much for an easy exit, Jenny thought, but to eavesdrop on any conversation in the bedroom.

No satisfaction for Anya on that score.

Jenny didn't even look at Dante, let alone speak to him. She rose from the bed and, finding her legs much steadier now, strolled over to the glass doors on the other side of the room to him. Outside was another colonnaded walkway, shading the area between this wing of the villa and the stone wall running along the cliff edge, beyond it the sea. She pretended to take in the view, her mind ferociously engaged on far more internal territory.

The sexuality Dante had aroused in her was still tingling through her body, making it feel vibrantly alive. Part of her wanted to pursue this experience with him, but what self-respect was there in that? The blonde bombshell in the bathroom represented his world—the beautiful people with money to burn. No doubt he'd poured out his famous charm to acquire her.

No charm for Jenny Kent. He was knowingly using his mega-strong physical attraction to get what he wanted from her. He'd probably been doing that with women all his life, given the male assets he'd been born with. Did she really want to fall victim to a cynical sexual play?

No.

It would be totally stupid of her.

Getting more deeply involved with Dante Rossini would only muddy what was already dangerous waters. She had to keep a clear head, not get distracted from what she had to do to earn her freedom.

'Got them,' Anya trilled, as though it had been a triumphant feat of discovery.

It struck a false note in the loaded silence.

Jenny turned to acknowledge her presence but didn't get a glance from the other woman. Anya's gaze was concentrated on Dante, who had remained by the opened bedroom door, pointedly waiting for her to depart.

'Then there's nothing to stop you from speeding on your way,' he drawled, dark eyes glittering impatience.

She flounced over to him, pausing to tilt up her beautiful face, pout her sexy mouth and say, 'I did apologise for the intrusion.'

'Curiosity killed the cat, Anya.' It was a cold indictment of her behaviour.

'I just wanted…'

'You've got what you came for. Go!'

His stony face did not invite argument. She left. He closed the door. Jenny steeled herself to rebuff any continuance of the scene Anya had interrupted. Dante turned to face her, his dark gaze skating over her stiff stance, his mouth curling into a twist of irony at the defensive wall so firmly back in place.

'Why don't you follow her?' Jenny flung at him. 'I don't need you to help me settle in here, and since you're obviously feeling some frustration, I'm sure your girlfriend would welcome the chance to ease it for you.'

'Ah, but I wouldn't welcome her efforts.'

Her heart skipped at the change of tone from icy distaste to seductive sensuality. It raced into a gallop as he started strolling towards her, his eyes mocking her attempt to reject what had happened between them.

'I don't welcome yours,' she stated vehemently. 'Your Casanova mentality doesn't appeal to me one bit.'

Her jeering contempt did not hold him back. He shrugged it off and kept on coming. 'Casanova romps are not my style. I'd decided to end my relationship with Anya before I flew to Australia for you.'

'She can't know that or she wouldn't be here.'

'Anya only listens to what she wants. Apparently my suggestion that she move on to another man made her think she'd better work harder to keep me, and she seized the opportunity Lucia held out to her.'

'Then let her work hard.' Anything to keep herself safe from what he could do to her!

He shook his head. 'I don't want her anymore.'

His eyes told her very graphically that she was now the object of desire. Jenny was hopelessly torn between her own secret desire for him to want her and the certain knowledge he intended to use sex to keep her in line with him. He wanted abject surrender from her, not a relationship that carried caring with it. He had no reason to care for her, never would.

'Don't look at me like that!' she cried. 'I've just seen the type of woman who attracts you and I'm not it. If you think you can fool me, think again!'

Dante did pause to think again. The fierce antagonism flowing from her would only deepen if he physically forced the issue. Persuasion was now the tactic to use to get her back to where he wanted her. And he did *want* her. The desire still surging through him was stronger than any he'd felt in a long time. Anya's sexual expertise was a tame thing compared to the powerhouse of passion he'd found in this woman.

He had to move Anya out of this villa, off Capri, get rid of that bone of contention before attempting another seduction, which would have to be carefully planned, given the level of resistance Anya's intrusion had forged.

'And get this straight,' the little spitfire hurled at him. 'I'll be Isabella for your grandfather whenever he wants my company, but I don't like

Lucia and Anya and I'm not going to mix with them when he's not there.'

'Anya will be gone before lunch.'

'Fine! Then you can lunch with your real cousin by yourself. Tell her I have a headache. Tell her I'm still suffering jetlag. Tell her anything you like to excuse me from having to put up with more stress, because I'm going to rest in this room all afternoon. *By myself.* Or I won't answer to how I conduct myself with your grandfather over dinner tonight,' she finished with threatening defiance.

'Good idea!' he approved, which instantly took the wind out of her battle sails. 'I'll have one of the maids bring you a tray of refreshments. Would you like headache pills, as well?'

She lifted a hand to push at her forehead. 'Yes, I would. Thank you,' she muttered, visibly sagging with relief at his response.

'Lucia can be a trial, but it will be impossible to completely avoid her,' he warned. 'I'll do my best to keep you apart. Okay?'

She nodded, looking too drained of energy to argue anymore.

'I'll leave you to rest.'

The deception had to be maintained at all costs, Dante reminded himself as he let himself out of the suite. It was probably reckless of him to pursue a sexual connection with his 'cousin.' In all honesty, he couldn't pass off this move as a means of winning her willing co-operation. He wanted to experience all of her.

The way she challenged him stirred his highly competitive instincts, driving a need to strip her of her armour, take her so totally she would concede everything to him. But he had to be careful, too, not incur any suspicion of the connection he intended to have with her. Control was paramount in this situation. He'd almost lost it, back there.

He smiled.

It didn't matter if he lost it behind closed doors.

CHAPTER NINE

HAD she made Dante think again?

Jenny stared at the closed door, not knowing if he'd decided that any further attempt at sexual domination was not a good idea, or if this was merely a reprieve. Her head *was* aching. She felt totally exhausted, her nerves frayed by an overload of tension. Whatever Dante intended, she was grateful he'd left her alone for a while, grateful not to have to be constantly thinking about what she had to say and do to remain safe in this place.

She dragged her gaze from the door and slowly swept it around the bedroom which was supposed to be her own private sanctuary. The fabrics used were mostly peaches and cream with touches of pale lime green. The furniture was white. Two armchairs and a coffee table holding a platter of fresh fruit were placed for the enjoyment of the view outside. A writing desk was graced by a beautiful arrangement of pastel carnations. A large plasma television set provided easy viewing from the bed which was king-size.

The room was so large, the big bed did not swamp the space, but it did swamp Jenny's mind with dark thoughts. It was so clearly a bed for two people, a bed for sex, a bed where Anya had lain with Dante, playing erotic games, using her lush femininity to keep him. What wiles would she try to make him reconsider his decision to end their relationship? Obviously she didn't want to let him go.

Would Dante reconsider, using a resumed affair with Anya to defray any suspicion of sexual interest in *his cousin*? He was certainly capable of doing anything to achieve what he wanted, Jenny reminded herself, hating her own vulnerability to the power of the man. Somehow she had to remain emotionally cold with him, not let him see he could get to her, though how she was going to manage that after losing her head with such mad passion she didn't know.

Sighing over the wretched mistake, she dragged her feet over to the door that led to the ensuite bathroom. Except it didn't directly. It opened to a short corridor which bisected the bathroom on one side and a dressing-room on the other, and at the end of it was another door. Shock squeezed her heart as she remembered this suite adjoined Dante's. He had private access to it. No one would see him if he chose to come to her at night.

She rushed over to try the door-knob. It didn't turn. Locked. But was there a key? Could he unlock it on his side? She fought down a wave of panic. There was nothing she could do about this now. When the maid came with the tray of refreshments, she could ask her about it, insist she be assured of absolute privacy.

Her head was throbbing. She needed to wash off her makeup and lie down. Her legs were shaky. She shoved herself back to the bathroom doorway. All her toiletries were neatly set out on a marble vanity bench. A glance back to the dressing room showed the rest of her luggage unpacked as well, clothes hanging up or stowed on shelves. Even her shoes had been stacked in pairs on a rack.

This was how the rich lived, she thought derisively, having everything done for them, having their wishes carried out, acquiring whatever they wanted, *including a grand-daughter.* How was she going to fill in these two months with the Rossini family, having nothing to do apart from chatting with Marco whenever he was well enough to want her company? Hiding in this suite day after day would be too unnatural. She couldn't see Dante allowing it. But at least he had left her to herself this afternoon.

She slept most of it away. When she woke it was almost five o'clock. Mercifully her headache was gone. A note had been slipped under her bedroom door. She picked it up with some trepidation, not knowing what to expect, but it was only a helpful list of instructions:

Call kitchen on telephone intercom for service when wanted.
Dinner is at eight.
Be ready by seven.
Wear Lisa Ho dress.

No signature but it had to be from Dante, doing his puppet-master thing again.

Having missed the two-o'clock lunch, and with dinner still three hours away, Jenny decided she needed some refuelling before her next performance. The platter of fruit did not appeal as much as a cup of coffee—a whole pot of coffee—so she called the kitchen and requested it, along with a serving of bruschetta. Her empty stomach was growling for something more substantial than grapes and peaches. It took a lot of energy and a sharp mind to keep on her toes with the Rossini family, and having to fight the perilous attraction to Dante took even more.

She tried not to fret over what might happen next with him. Nevertheless, it was impossible to suppress some anxiety as the meeting time approached. She had eaten, showered, dressed, made up her face in appropriate tones to complement the green and gold hues in the filmy, frilly, ultra-feminine Lisa Ho creation, put on the gold jewellery, fluffed up her hair, was satisfied that she was presentable, then had nothing to do in the last twenty minutes, except pace around the room and worry about things she couldn't control.

Getting some fresh air seemed like a better activity. She opened the glass doors, crossed the colonnaded walkway and leaned against the stone wall, breathing in the salty scent of the sea and watching the shifting colour of sky and water as the sun set. The seeking of some peace of mind was short-lived. She'd barely started to relax when Dante's voice snapped her back to full-on tension.

'I hope you're not thinking of jumping.'

The sardonic drawl seemed to crawl down her spine. Her heart leapt into a jitter-bug. She gritted her teeth and fiercely told herself not to get rattled, to adopt a cool aloofness that denied she was in any way affected by his presence.

'I'm not yet defeated by life,' she replied, turning to see him stepping out of *her* bedroom, which was an instant reminder of the set-up he'd orchestrated. 'Did you just use the connecting door between our suites?'

He shrugged as though it was totally inconsequential. 'I knocked first. When there was no response, I thought I'd better check on you.'

It sounded reasonable but Jenny glared her dislike of the too intimate situation. She'd decided not to fuss about having a key, realising he either had one or could acquire one, and making a fuss to anyone else might raise eyebrows over questions of trust where there should be none, not between *cousins*.

'Don't assume you can invade my privacy any time you like, Dante,' she said tersely.

His mouth twitched into a smile as he crossed the walkway to the stone wall, his gaze flicking down and up, assessing her overall appearance. 'I see you're in fine form again. Headache gone?'

'Yes, thank you.'

She whipped her gaze back to the view when he joined her at the wall, standing too close for comfort. He was wearing a white suit and an open-necked black shirt—a striking combination that oozed sex appeal on him. She was so acutely conscious of his nearness she could barely breathe, and her mind's eye was so occupied with his image the sunset was a blur. It was an act of will to keep her voice working in a fairly natural tone.

'Who will be at dinner tonight?' she asked, more fixated on Anya's presence than anyone else's, torn between wanting her gone and needing to have Dante's sexual drive diverted away from herself.

'Just Nonno and his three grandchildren. He's been resting all afternoon, as well, looking forward to this evening. I trust we'll have a pleasant dinner together.'

A touch of steel was added to his voice on those last words—a warning to behave as he wanted her to behave with Marco. Remembering his other warning, she couldn't stop herself from mockingly asking, 'Has Anya paid for not pleasing you?'

'Oh, I think Anya profited quite well from our relationship,' he said cynically. 'Which is why she wanted to extend it past its use-by date. I told her in no uncertain terms that I'm not interested in an extension, and she flew back to Rome this afternoon. With *all* her toiletries.'

Gone…

Jenny didn't know if she was disappointed or relieved. One source of possibly hostile attention had been eliminated, making the situation less complicated on the social level. On the other hand, Anya's departure meant she couldn't be used as a line of defence against any disturbing move Dante made on her.

She shot him a hard look. 'Have you always ordered your world how you want it?'

He grimaced. 'If I could do that, my mother and father would still be alive, and Nonno wouldn't be dying of cancer.'

'Family,' she murmured, thinking it was the one thing he couldn't choose.

'My parents died when I was six,' he went on. 'Nonno took me under his wing. He was always there for me. He's given me so much, I had to give him you, Isabella. I couldn't tell him you were dead, not when he's dying.'

Was it an appeal for understanding? Another play for her co-operation? Ruthless blackmail, sexual connection, a pull on her emotional strings…anything and everything was grist for his mill.

Yet maybe it wasn't ego driving him. Maybe he was half-crazed by grief at the imminent loss of the grandfather who had nurtured and supported him since he was a little boy.

She shouldn't have taken over Bella's identity. None of this would have happened if she hadn't made that decision—taken when her mind had been torn by grief for her friend and desperation on her own account. Impossible to imagine then she was setting up a collision course with Dante Rossini and would end up here, paying for that decision. And maybe it was right that she should pay for it. Marco's investigators had been deceived into reporting Isabella was alive. Her fault.

She heaved a regretful sigh. 'I'm sorry I caused this mess. I *will* do my best to give your grandfather what he needs from Bella, Dante. You don't need to…to force more from me.'

A rush of hot embarrassment burned her cheeks. She hadn't fought his kisses. It shamed her that her response to them had not been negative. Dante wasn't likely to forget that explosive passion. Her mind squirmed over it, wondering if she could explain it away, say it had erupted from anger, nothing at all to do with an attraction that was still tearing at her, despite common sense dictating how dangerously stupid it was.

She stared out to sea, painfully aware he had swung towards her and was studying her profile. Did he believe her? Would he trust her to continue behaving as Bella might have done? Her skin kept burning under the intensity of his probing gaze. He made her so tense she could hardly think.

'Who were your parents?'

The soft curious tone washed through her jangling mind like cool water. The relief from hot pressure was so great, she forgot about denying him information about herself. It seemed harmless to tell him the truth, easier than prolonging a silence that fed her fears.

'I don't know. No one does. I was an abandoned baby, only a few hours old when I was found. Public appeals were made for the mother to come forward, but she never did.'

'Probably a student,' he mused. 'For whatever reason, she must have had to hide her pregnancy, hide the fact she'd had a baby.'

Surprised by this sympathetic reading from him, she shot him a quizzical look. 'Why do you say that? Why not someone who simply didn't want to be loaded with me, who didn't want to bother with the fuss of handing me over to officials for adoption?'

'Someone who didn't care would have had an

abortion.' He shook his head. 'I think your mother was very young and had a lot to lose by admitting to the mistake of getting pregnant, but you were her flesh and blood and she couldn't bring herself to deny you life.'

She frowned at his persistence in drawing this picture of her unknown mother, whom Jenny had privately condemned for dumping her baby daughter in a limbo of not belonging anywhere. 'I don't know why you're going on about her like this. It makes no difference to what happened to me. No parents. No family. The nurses at the hospital named me Jenny and I was found in Kent Street. There you have it. Jenny Kent.'

His question was answered.

But he didn't let it drop.

The speculative interest in his eyes didn't even waver.

'I believe genetic inheritance contributes far more to one's character than environment. I think your mother was a student because you're remarkably intelligent. I think she felt trapped and scared, and just as you denied your own identity to survive, she denied being a mother to survive.'

'I'd never give up a child of mine,' she cried emphatically, resenting the parallel he was drawing.

'No, I don't think you would,' he said in measured judgement. 'That's where environment comes in. I doubt your mother had the experience of being an abandoned child herself. But in traumatic situations, people do make decisions they later regret.'

Like me, coming out of the coma, faced with too many problems to cope with.

Maybe she should think more kindly of her mother. What was the old saying? 'Don't judge people until you've walked a mile in their shoes?'

It suddenly struck her how strange this conversation with Dante was. What was the purpose behind it? Why would he care how she thought about her mother? It had nothing to do with his high-powered life, nothing to do with…

'Like my grandfather turning his back on his youngest son,' he added quietly. 'Then it becomes too late to turn back the clock.'

Ah! He was setting up a more sympathetic bond between her and Marco, tapping into her own background to establish an emotional link, pulling strings again. Had he decided the sexual angle might be too volatile to be safely handled? Was she off that hook?

She turned and looked him straight in the eye. 'I said I'd do my best, Dante. I meant it.'

His long, hard, assessing stare was difficult to hold, making Jenny feel stretched on a rack with him tightening the screws, testing every nerve in her body. Nevertheless, she was determined on making him believe her and it was not her gaze that dropped first.

It was his.

Slowly sliding down to her mouth, stopping there.

And she knew he wasn't thinking about the words it had just delivered. He was remembering how she had responded to his kisses, wanting to test the memory, relive it.

Her breath caught in her throat. Her heart hammered her chest. Her stomach contracted. Tremors ran down her thighs. One hand gripped the edge of the stone wall, fingers spread wide for supporting traction. The other curled into a fist. Her mind screamed not to show weakness, to fight him off if he touched her.

He didn't move. His gaze lifted to hers again, dark eyes simmering with a sensuality that sent a convulsive little shiver down her spine. Fear or excitement she didn't know, couldn't let herself think about it. He was so damnably sexy and his eyes were promising pleasure she'd never get with anyone else.

'You look so beautiful tonight, Nonno will be proud to own you as his grand-daughter,' he said huskily. 'He'll put aside the fact there is nothing of Antonio in you. That's half the battle won. The rest should be easy as long as you're committed to it.'

Her breath released itself in a shaky sigh. 'I am,' she assured him, feeling she had just been given another reprieve.

He smiled, the warm satisfaction in his eyes making her skin tingle. It was impossible to stop her body reacting to this man.

He gestured an invitation to move. 'Shall we stroll along the walkway to the terrace? We can go from there through the atrium to the entertainment wing of the villa.'

Game on again, Jenny thought as she set out with him, trying to direct her mind away from its acute awareness of the physical chemistry that seemed to buzz between them. 'What reception am I likely to get from Lucia this time?' she asked.

'All sweetness and light under Nonno's eye,' he answered dryly.

'How did she take Anya's departure?'

'Oh, she put on a fine act of having misunderstood the situation, believing she was doing me a good turn in inviting Anya here. Lucia is an expert at cutting her losses when she no longer sees any advantage for herself in holding a stand.'

'You sound very cynical about her.'

He shrugged. 'It's just the way she is. Aunt Sophia has veered between indulging her and neglecting her. Lucia worked out how to manipulate her mother and everyone else around her at a very young age. It annoys the hell out of her that I see straight through her games.'

'Being a master game player yourself.'

His eyes glittered acknowledgement of that truth. 'It's how one stays on top.'

Ruthless control, Jenny thought.

And couldn't help wondering what it would be like to feel all that power in bed with him.

CHAPTER TEN

THEY dined in a room overlooking a fabulous swimming pool. Underwater lights gave the water a blue brilliance and sparkled through a glorious fountain at the far end. Statues of Roman gods stood in the surrounding grounds amongst trellises of grapevines and urns of flowers. The outlook was so stunning, Jenny's gaze was drawn to it every time there was a lull in the conversation. It provided relief from the tension of having to be Bella with every word she spoke.

She wasn't so much under the gun from Marco Rossini tonight. He seemed content to sit back, watch and listen while Lucia directed a barrage of questions at her new cousin, most of which were easy to handle.

'Do you have a boyfriend waiting for you back home?' was thrown at her after the main course had been cleared away.

'No. What about you? Do you have one?'

A careless shrug. 'No one special. I can pick up anyone I want whenever I want.'

The arrogance of great wealth, Jenny thought. Dante probably had the same attitude. Discarding Anya had not worried him one bit. No emotional involvement. She'd do well to remember that.

'What do you do with your time when you're on your own?' Lucia carried on.

'I draw. Or paint.'

'What do you draw?'

'Portraits mostly.' It gave her a perverse kind of pleasure to shock Lucia with the truth. 'I've been what you'd call a street artist. People who come to the Venetian Forum in Sydney pay me to do a portrait of them on the spot.'

'*Dio!* That's not much better than a beggar!'

'I like it. There are so many interesting faces.

Like Dante's.' She smiled at him, revelling in rebelling against caution for once. 'I wanted to sketch it before he asked me to.'

'Dante asked a cheap street artist to do a portrait of him?' Lucia sounded scandalised by such a lowly activity.

His dark eyes stabbed a warning at Jenny that she was playing with fire before turning a bland look to Lucia. 'It was my first meeting with Bella. I wanted to get to know her at least a little before identifying myself and telling her why I had come.'

'I'd like to see the portrait,' Marco said, drawing everyone's attention to him. His eyes sparkled with interest, dark pinpoints of vitality in a face that looked almost grey with fatigue or pain. 'Did you bring it home with you, Dante?'

'No,' he said ruefully.

'I didn't finish it,' Jenny explained. 'When he told me who he was…'

'She packed up her things and stormed away from me, wanting nothing to do with any of us,' he finished dryly.

'Why ever not?' Lucia cried in disbelief.

'Because we were of no significance in her life…and should have been,' Marco answered heavily. He turned to Jenny in appeal. 'Perhaps you would do a portrait of Dante for me while you're here.'

She shrugged an apology. 'I didn't bring any art materials with me.'

'No matter. I will supply them.' He turned to his grandson. 'You'll see to it, won't you, Dante? Everything Bella needs for her drawing and painting, now that she is staying with us.'

'First thing tomorrow, Nonno,' he promised.

'Just a sketchpad and some sticks of charcoal will do,' Jenny put in anxiously, not wanting to accept any more from them.

Marco waved a dismissive hand at her protest. 'What artist would not want to capture the colour of Capri? You do me the favour of giving me your company. Let me give you the pleasure of doing what you like doing while you're here. Get everything, Dante,' he repeated, not to be denied on this point.

It *would* fill in the hours…days…weeks… months…

Jenny grabbed the idea with gratitude, realising it would provide her with an escape from both Dante's company and Lucia's. She could be herself in her own world for as long as she was occupied with art.

She smiled at the old man. 'Thank you. I would enjoy trying my hand at doing some landscapes.'

He smiled back. 'And I will enjoy seeing you happy at work.'

'Have you sold any of your paintings?' Lucia asked with a lofty air, clearly peeved by her grandfather's indulgence towards the new grand-daughter and wanting to downgrade the talent being indulged.

'Yes. But not for very much,' Jenny answered, quite happy to downplay herself since it was the truth.

A condescending little smile played across Lucia's mouth. 'I know one of the top gallery owners in Rome. If I asked him, he'd be happy to give you an opinion of your work.'

Jenny shook her head. 'Thank you, but I'm not up to that standard.'

'Oh!' It was almost a sneer.

'Bella is planning to get some formal training next year,' Marco said, a slight reproof in his voice. 'It's time you thought of putting some structure in *your* life, Lucia, furthering your education so you can pursue a more rewarding occupation than attending parties.'

'They are fund-raisers for charities,' she quickly justified.

'Charities are better served by work,' came the terse reply.

Lucia gestured a pretty appeal. 'What would you have me do, Nonno? Just tell me…'

'Find some drive within yourself that gives you satisfaction,' he answered wearily. 'I can't tell you what it is.'

'But I'm absolutely satisfied with my life,' she blithely argued.

'Then you are cheaply satisfied, my dear, and you'll end up like your mother, being exploited by others.'

'No one will ever exploit me,' she retorted in gritty anger. 'I've seen what happens with my mother and I've learnt from it.'

'Sophia has nothing to fall back on, nothing to fill the emptiness when it comes,' he said sadly. 'You should find something for yourself, something that can always give you a sense of personal achievement, Lucia. That's what I'm telling you. This will never be a problem for

Dante. I doubt it will ever be a problem for Bella. But you risk losing yourself in meaningless pursuits unless you find a more solid direction for your life.'

The long speech drained him. He sucked in breath and gestured to Dante. 'Take me to my suite. Must rest.'

Lucia leapt to her feet. 'I can help you, Nonno.'

He waved her down. 'Dante.'

There was no arguing with that firm edict.

His caregiver had brought him to dinner in a wheelchair, evidence that he hadn't felt well enough to walk. Not well enough to eat much, either. He'd been served only small portions of the pasta entrée and the main veal dish, most of which had been pushed around his plate. As Dante wheeled him away from the table, it really shot home to Jenny that time was running out for Marco Rossini. He was dying, perhaps faster than the doctors had predicted.

Be kind to him...

She took Dante's request to heart at that moment, silently vowing to give his grandfather whatever pleasure she could. Tomorrow she would try her best to capture the essence of Dante in a portrait.

No sooner had the two men left the room than a maid came in, carrying the sweets course—small balls of different flavoured sorbets, easy for Marco to eat, Jenny thought, except he wasn't here anymore. The maid hesitated at the absence of half the dinner party.

'Serve us and take the rest back,' Lucia commanded snippishly, still put out at having her help rejected.

Jenny waited until the maid had departed, then attempted to reduce Lucia's smouldering annoyance. 'Dante told me he'd been with his grandfather since he was six. It's only natural…'

'Oh, shut up!' The dark eyes blazed absolute fury. 'You might have won over Dante and Nonno with your smarmy, agree-with-everything act, but I know what you're after.'

'I'm not *after* anything,' Jenny stated emphatically, feeling her own temperature starting to rise.

'A clever card to play,' Lucia jeered. 'It worked on my mother every time—lovers who didn't go after her for the money, except they took her big-time once she fell for it. It's quite marvellous how you didn't want anything to do with us, yet here you are, feeding Nonno a guilt-trip about you so he'll bend over backwards to give you everything he can.'

Jenny took a deep breath, telling herself to stay calm. 'I'm sorry you've learnt to be so cynical about people, Lucia,' she said reasonably, 'but you're wrong about me. I...'

'I don't have any art materials with me,' she mimicked mockingly. 'It was a deadset certainty that Nonno would supply you with the best range of stuff that can be bought. Not a bad start, Bella.'

The acid sarcasm bit. 'I won't keep it. It's just for here. I'll leave it all behind when I go home.'

Lucia's eyes lit with malevolent triumph. 'So the art thing is an act, too. No wonder you didn't want an expert opinion on your work.'

'No, it's not an act,' Jenny retorted heatedly. 'I have my own stuff at home. I don't need to take anything from your grandfather. And I won't!'

'Only the inheritance that would have gone to your papa. Don't tell me that's not on your mind.'

'It's not. But even if it were, why should it matter to you? What will you lose by it? Aren't there enough Rossini billions to go around for you? How much do you need, Lucia?'

'It's not the damned money!' She slammed her hands down on the table and stood up, leaning forward to spit vicious words at Jenny. 'You arrive here, thick as thieves with Dante, and Nonno immediately takes to you, even throws you in my face as an example of how I should lead my life. As if he's ever cared about my life!'

'He's just shown you he cares,' Jenny pointed out quietly, realising Lucia was fuming with jealousy.

'He's never done anything for me!' That was fired straight back at her. Her hands sliced the air in exasperated fury. 'It's always been Dante, Dante, Dante. His precious grandson got all his attention while I was dragged around the world by my mother, different minders, different schools, whatever suited her convenience.'

Her hands slammed down on the table again, eyes burning with hatred. 'Do you know how many times I wished I was an orphan so Nonno would take me in and give me what he gave Dante? And now he's found another orphaned grandchild to shower his attention on.'

Jenny shook her head. 'He's dying, Lucia. I won't have much time with him.'

'It should be *my* time. I wish he hadn't found you. I wish you were dead like your parents.'

'Lucia!'

Dante's voice thundered across the room as the blood drained from Jenny's face. Bella *was* dead...*was* dead...had been dead these past six months. She had no right to be here, taking up time that a real grand-daughter should have.

'Don't think you can order me to leave, Dante!' his cousin yelled, the harsh decibels in her voice hurting Jenny's ears. 'This villa isn't yours yet! I have as much right as you to say and do whatever I like.'

'If abusing people is your style, do it to an empty room. I won't have Bella subjected to your spite.' He strode over to Jenny, hauled her up from her chair, tucking her protectively to his side, a strong arm around her shoulders.

'Right! Run off together!' Lucia jeered. 'I've always been alone anyway. Nothing new there.'

'Try thinking of others instead of how every-thing affects *you,* and you might have a differ-ent result. Wishing Bella dead because it would suit you better is beyond contempt.'

The lash of his voice brought scarlet flags to Lucia's cheeks. 'I wish you were dead, too,' she said venomously.

'You always have. But you know what, Lucia? I've never once complained to Nonno about the malicious traps you've set for me. But try it on with Bella and I *will* tell him what a nasty piece of work you are. He doesn't have much tolerance for wrong-doing. He banished his own son so completely, we didn't even know of his existence until a week ago.'

The power of that threat hung in the silence that followed it—a silence loaded with violent emotion, barely held in check. Dante swept Jenny out of the room, her legs feeling as wooden as a marionette's, her mind pummelled by a dreadful sense of wrong-doing. She should never have agreed to this deception. There were too many repercussions to it. Dante had tunnel vision if he thought it was as simple as granting a deathbed wish. Nothing about it was simple.

'Don't fold on me now,' Dante muttered fiercely, sensing the turbulence weakening her earlier commitment to staying on here, almost carrying her down the long corridor to their bedroom suites, enveloping her with his own strength of purpose so she couldn't break away.

Once inside her room he locked the door against any possible intrusion, but he didn't release his hold on her. Before Jenny could say a word, she found herself locked in his embrace, her head gently pressed onto his broad shoulder, his hand stroking through her hair with soothing intent, his mouth warmly brushing her ear, his breath wafting over it as he spoke, his voice a deep rumble that rolled through her, making her feel even more shaky.

'There's no turning back. Whatever Lucia said to you, it makes no difference.'

She should be fighting the dominating power he was exerting, yet she couldn't summon the strength to do it. There was comfort in being held so tightly, being stroked, feeling his caring about the stress she'd been put through. Tears spilled into her eyes. Tears of weakness. She didn't want to stand alone. Her whole body craved this seductive togetherness with him. Though part of her torn mind insisted that his caring was centred on protecting his own interests, wanting her to keep doing what he wanted.

She swallowed hard, blinked back the tears and forced herself to say, 'Yes, it does. It does make it different. I'm taking time away from her. Time that shouldn't be mine. And since I was the one who created this situation, I should take the blame for it. I'll tell your grandfather and Lucia I deceived you about being Bella. That won't bring you down in their eyes, Dante.'

It didn't matter what happened to her. Not meaning to do any harm did not excuse the wrong she'd done. She was filled with guilty shame and didn't want to live with it any longer.

His fingers entwined themselves in her hair, gently tugging her head up from his shoulder. She wanted to keep her eyes closed but the need to let him see she'd spoken the truth forced her to open them, to meet his dark questing gaze without any wavering.

He stared at her. For long, nerve-wracking moments, his eyes burned into hers as though they were scorching a path to her innermost soul. She was suddenly acutely conscious of the tension in his body, the pressure of his thighs against hers, the arm around her waist holding her firmly pinned to him, her breasts crushed against the hard hot wall of his chest.

Her heart started hammering.

The expression in his eyes changed to a glitter of satisfaction as though he sensed the loss of focus in her concentration on the deception issue and liked the physical awareness of him much better. 'I don't want to let you go, and you don't want me to, either,' he said with arrogant certainty.

He kissed her.

And she let him do it, knowing it was foolish, yet overwhelmingly tempted to feel whatever he could make her feel, before she returned to her own life. She'd never known a man like him, never would again. Only extraordinary circumstances had brought about this connection and it had to end, but she could take one night with him away with her.

Recklessly abandoning any sense of caution, she kissed him back, wanting to incite the explosion of passion that had blown her mind earlier today. He tasted her surrender, revelled in it, his mouth plundering hers for more and more of her giving, as though he couldn't get enough of it, and the wild intoxication of his need drove her own for more of him.

Excitement pumped through her body. His was moving sensuously against hers, making her aware of the excitement pulsing through him, making her crave the power of his sexuality. She wanted to be taken by him. He stirred something terribly primitive in her, a rampant desire to possess the essence of the man, to hold him in *her* power, if only for a little time.

Her arms were still by her sides. Her hands dragged up and down his hard muscular thighs, blindly transmitting the need that was clawing through her. A convulsive little thrill ran down her spine as his fingers burrowed through her hair to the zipper at the back of the designer dress and drew it down, baring her skin to his touch.

His mouth broke from hers, muttering something in Italian. His face wore a look of urgent intensity, his eyes blazing a command for her to remain exactly where she was while his hands worked quickly at stripping her of the fine feathers he'd clothed her in.

Yes, Jenny thought fiercely, wanting to be shed of the designer image, which was all part and parcel of the deception, wanting to feel free of everything, just be the woman she was, naked with nothing, and still being desired by Dante Rossini. His hands and mouth assured her this was true…long, shivery caresses down her back, over her buttocks, hot intimate caresses, kisses drawing her breasts into throbbing peaks, kisses on her stomach, her thighs. She was awash with exciting sensation.

Then he was surging up to his full towering height again, tearing off his own clothes, and she silently exulted in his wild haste, her eyes feasting on the magnificent maleness being revealed: satin-smooth olive skin, stretched tightly over perfect muscles, his whole physique in pleasing and heart-pummelling proportion. She could barely wait to run her hands over him, to feel his nakedness against hers. He was a beautiful man—his face, his body, the aggressive energy emanating from him, flooding her with an intense sense of being the weaker sex.

Which probably should have frightened her, but it didn't. It made her feel very female, meltingly soft, her whole being yearning for his hard strength to envelop her, fill her, take her to places she had never been, places she'd read about but never experienced in the few unsatisfying sexual encounters she'd had in the past. This man was different. She knew it in her bones, knew it from the uncontrollable responses he drew from her, knew it from the most basic of basic instincts.

He picked her up and carried her to the bed like a caveman claiming his woman. Her arms were around his neck, hands wantonly kneading the taut muscles in his back, her breasts crushed to the heaving wall of his chest, glorying in the silky heat of his naked skin. He knelt between her legs as he lowered her onto the bed, hovering over her like some dark beast of prey intent on devouring her, and she laughed at her own wild imagination, laughed with a mad joy in his ravenous desire for her.

He choked off her laugh with a long, driving kiss that turned her joy to a feverish passion. She wound her legs around his hips, her feet stroking his legs, pushing at them, goading him to act. The kiss was not enough. It promised. It incited. It tantalised. But it didn't deliver what she wanted, needed, her whole body screaming to feel him deep inside her, deeper than the kiss, much deeper.

She arched in sheer ecstacy when he finally entered her, plunging hard and fast to the place that had been waiting to welcome him, the place that pulsed with intense pleasure at his filling of the void, so brilliantly intense she could hardly bear it. He retreated from it, then came again, and again, and again, building an exquisite tension that splintered into sweet chaos, bringing wave after wave of euphoria crashing through her entire body.

And still he came, stroking through the waves, riding the crests, sucked into the honeyed heart of her, until he, too, spiralled beyond all control, spilling himself in great spasms, a stream of life eddying and swirling, hot, urgent, gloriously ful-filling her wish to possess some of him…if only for a little while.

She held him to her, filling all her senses with

him, smelling the musky scent of after-sex, listening to his ragged breathing, feeling the thumping beat of his heart, seeing the glisten of sweat on his skin, loving the intimacy of it all. He rolled onto his back, carrying her with him, his arms holding her just as tightly, tucking her head under his chin, making her feel like his cherished possession.

It was as though they were cocooned together in a silent world of their own, content to be as one in it. She knew it had to end soon, knew they had to be parted, but not yet…

Please…not yet.

Let this night be long.

One night…before tomorrow.

CHAPTER ELEVEN

DANTE stretched his legs over hers, squeezed the lush roundness of her bottom, entwined the tangled curls of her hair around his fingers, holding her tightly in his grasp. No way was he about to let her slip away from him. She was something else…this woman.

Apart from stirring the animal in him, she had one hell of a strong pull on his mind. He was used to women in the Anya mould—women who counted the score, knowing how to work the wealthy social scene, giving enough to get what they wanted. Despite Jenny Kent's different background, he'd still assumed she'd fall in with his plan. It was in her best interests to do so. Yet she was bucking his judgement at every turn.

She cared about deceiving his grandfather.

She cared about deceiving Lucia.

She cared about taking what wasn't rightly hers to take, though she had taken over Bella's identity. As a short-term survival measure, she'd told him. Reasonable enough in the circumstances when she'd believed it wouldn't hurt anyone.

And now she didn't want to hurt him—the man who'd forced her into this situation—prepared to shoulder the whole fraudulent conspiracy herself rather than take him down with her.

Amazing that she cared so much for others.

But she didn't realise her confession would not serve any good whatsoever. Lucia would go on being a spoilt brat, making as much capital as she could out of *the mistake*, crowing over Nonno's disappointment instead of trying to assuage it by being the kind of grand-daughter that gave him what he wanted given to him. Impossible anyway. Only Bella could do that— Jenny being Bella.

The status quo had to be maintained.

Besides, he wanted more of this woman.

Much more.

Right now she lay passively in his embrace. *Physically* passive. Passion spent. He wondered what had driven such wild passion in her. This hadn't been an act of seduction, though he'd meant it to be whatever was needed to keep her on track. From the moment he kissed her…it had to have been a wilful decision or an irresist-ible impulse on her part to embrace the strong chemistry between them, give it free expres-sion. There'd been no inhibitions to overcome.

Maybe for her it was a release from all the tension he'd put her through this past week—a physical venting of all the feelings she'd kept bottled up behind her wall of silence. And, of course, he was the focus of those feelings, having forced her into this high-pressure situation.

No matter. The sex had been unbelievably fantastic. Which was all to the good. Except… he suspected that sex, however fantastic it was, would not hold her against her will. It could be that she'd let herself have it—taking it from him—because tomorrow she would be gone.

Dante gritted his teeth in determination.

One way or another, he had to make her stay.

He'd try pushing the sex first.

He unclenched his jaw, forced himself to relax, then slowly and languorously rolled her onto her back, propped himself on his side, and gently stroked her hair back from her face, smiling into the eyes that fluttered open, looking at him with an expression of anxious wariness.

'Tell me why you laughed,' he invited, using a tone of indulgent curiosity.

It surprised her into a reminiscent smile. 'It's so mad…you and me.'

'But right at that moment you didn't care.'

'No. I didn't.'

'Neither did I.'

Her smile turned wry. 'A one-off thing for both of us.'

'I don't want it to be.' His gaze dropped to her mouth as he ran feather-light fingers over her lips. 'I haven't had nearly enough of you.'

She breathed in hard, knocked his hand away and spoke with fierce pride. 'I might be a nobody with nothing to my name, but don't think you can keep me as your secret little whore, Dante. I had sex with you because I wanted to but I'm not staying around for more of it.'

He raised a mocking eyebrow. 'Not good enough for you?'

She flushed. 'That's not the point.'

'It is to me. I can't recall ever having had it so good.' He glided his hand down her throat to her breasts, caressing them as though there were exquisite to his touch. Which they were. Even more so because of her reluctance to concede to him. 'Can you say differently?' he purred, confident of her response.

Confusion swirled in her eyes. 'That's not the point,' she repeated with an edge of desperation. 'I don't belong in your world. You know I don't.'

'My world is what I make it. I've already made you part of it.'

'As your cousin. A cousin you shouldn't be touching.'

'We both know that isn't true so we're not doing anything wrong. Why not enjoy what we can have together?' He reached down to the hot moist cleft between her legs, gently stroking a reminder of how intimately they had connected. 'It's about mutual pleasure, which is so far removed from your being degraded by the two of us being lovers that it's absurd for you to think like that. Secrecy will have to be maintained but I would never view you as selling yourself to me. It's not in your nature. You'd be milking this situation for all you could get if that was your mindset.'

'The situation is wrong, Dante,' she argued, her breathing quickening at the excitement his fingers were slowly re-igniting.

'No,' he quickly assured her. 'You're providing my grandfather with a distraction from his pain, giving him an outlet for memories he wants to open up before he dies. Only your presence can soothe the feelings of guilt he has over banishing his son.'

'But I'm not Bella.'

It was a cry of anguish.

Dante leaned over and tenderly grazed his lips over hers, wanting to soothe the turmoil in her mind. 'Whatever kind of person Bella was, you do her credit by being the person you are in her place. You're doing good.'

She grabbed his face, lifting it to make him look into eyes that were still pained. 'It hurts

Lucia. I'm taking your grandfather's attention away from her and she has the right to it.'

Anger boiled up in him and with it a surge of aggression. He ceased the intimate caressing, lifting his hand to her chin, holding it firmly as he inserted his leg between hers and half-covered her body, instinctively using physical dominance to add pressure to his claim on her mind.

'Lucia…' he snarled contemptuously, his eyes blazing a conviction that couldn't be refuted. 'What was she doing this past week when she could have had all Nonno's attention? Off shopping in Rome and fixing a visit from Anya. Does that speak of a need to be with her grandfather to you?'

No answer. She stared up at him but the lack of sharp focus in her eyes told him his argument was registering in her mind. All he had to do was nail it home to her.

'Lucia could have spent that time reaching out to Nonno if that's what she really wanted. But no. She likes the power of playing her games with people and you were her target tonight, putting you down, stirring you up, making you feel like an unwanted interloper. And she was doing that to Bella, remember. Bella, your friend. Your friend who was like a sister to you. She had no right to do that. No right at all. How would Bella have felt if she'd been here?'

She frowned, not liking the reality of what her friend might have faced.

'It was cruel,' he hammered in. 'And if you let Lucia win, you'll hurt my grandfather, not her. She'd be preening over your departure, having scored a hit against me for having brought you here, never mind how Nonno would feel about it. And he's the one who counts. The only one. This is *his* time—the little time he has left—and he chooses to have you with him. You…'

He kissed her, trying to tease a response, but it wasn't there.

'You with your caring,' he murmured, and slid

his tongue between her lips, wanting her to open up to him. Which she did, but passively, her mind still too full of other things.

'You with your giving,' he pressed, kissing her more deeply, using all his erotic expertise to get her focus back on what *they* could share together while she was Bella.

Her grip on his face eased, fingers sliding into his hair. Elation buzzed through him as her tongue slowly tangled with his. He'd won, and the win fired his desire for what she could give *him*. He wanted to feel the fire in her, wanted to build it to white-hot passion again, so he concentrated on keeping control this time, revelling in pleasuring her, feeding her sensuality with a slow journey of kisses and caresses all over her body, exulting as she squirmed in heat, when she clawed his back, wildly wanting the ultimate completion of his flesh plunged into hers.

Her need heightened his, the first deep thrust inside her feeling like a sunburst of incredible satisfaction. Control instantly evaporated. She made him feel like a great eagle, soaring and swooping, riding currents of air that zinged with sensation. It was brilliant, flying towards the highest of highs and she was taking him there, bucking and squeezing, drawing him on until he was utterly driven by her journey to the peak of ecstacy, reaching it with her, exploding like a nova that radiated out from the molten inner core of her to every cell in his body.

His mind was gone.

His strength was gone.

He floated in a weird kind of vacuum where she was the only anchor. Eventually his senses returned and he realised his body-weight must be crushing her, yet her arms were wound around him as though she didn't want him to move, or couldn't bear to break the closeness. He didn't want to break it, either, but he raised himself enough to kiss her forehead, her closed eyelids, her nose, her lips, and whisper, 'Say you'll stay.'

He breathed in her breath as she answered, 'Yes.'

He'd won.

She'd surrendered to his will.

And through him ran a sense of triumph that was sweeter than any he'd known.

CHAPTER TWELVE

JENNY sat at the newly acquired easel which had been set up close to Marco's sun-lounge on the terrace so he could watch her attempt to capture his grandson in charcoal. His caregiver, Theresa Farmilo, a middle-aged private nurse with a kindly manner, sat on the other side of him, ready to attend to his needs. A large umbrella shaded all three of them from the late-morning sun.

Dante was seated at the table, a few metres away, shaded by another umbrella. She'd asked him to chat with his grandfather, rather than hold a still pose. Silence and being the focus of all attention would have made her more nervous about doing the portrait. Besides, the vitality of his face when he talked was more interesting to work on than a simple sketch of flesh and bone and hair. More challenging, too.

He was an extremely challenging man. She no longer had any clear idea of what was right or wrong. He'd swamped her with intense sexual pleasure last night, argued her out of her concern for Lucia, re-asserted the need to indulge his grandfather with Bella's presence, and she had been unable to find the will to deny him anything.

Just do what he wants, kept running through her mind. It was too hard to fight him. Besides, this was his family and his judgement of it had to be better than hers. Though what Lucia had revealed about her life still touched a chord of sympathy—no settled home, a stream of minders, the lack of any deep personal interest being shone on her. In a weird kind of way, it echoed Jenny's own life. Wealth didn't really make up for the sense of inner loneliness. It only meant basic survival was never an issue.

Maybe she could speak to Marco about Lucia when they had some private time together, without Dante listening and butting in. If she could do some good there she would feel better about staying. Though Lucia might resent her interference, however well meant it was. Jenny had not seen her this morning, had no idea if she was ashamed of last night's cruel outburst or didn't care what hurt she had inflicted. No doubt their next meeting would reveal more of her nature. Best to wait and see.

More troubling than the question of Lucia was the new intimacy with Dante. She hadn't planned to have a prolonged secret affair with him. Her intention had been to end everything this morning. Now he clearly expected them to continue being cousins during the day and lovers at night—another deception that didn't sit easily in her mind. Yet her body was saying *yes* to it, regardless of how stupid and reckless it was to get so deeply involved with him.

Here she was, studying his mouth to draw it right, and all she could think of was how it had kissed her…everywhere. Just looking at him stirred a host of exciting memories. He'd said he wanted more of her and she couldn't deny wanting more of him. If he came to her room tonight, she knew she wouldn't be able to refuse him.

This was time out of time, she told herself. A brief madness that would end when Marco died. Then she would return to her real life, and her connection to Dante Rossini would seem like a dream. She hoped she would be able to remember it with a smile—an experience that would never have come her way in the ordinary course of events. In the meantime she had to keep filling the grand-daughter role, make sure she didn't get anything too wrong.

The pleasant peace on the terrace was interrupted just as Jenny was putting the last touches to the portrait.

'Good morning, all!' Lucia trilled, arriving via the cliff walkway, obviously having enjoyed a recent swim in the pool. She wore a red bikini, the bottom half covered by a matching sarong, and a large, floppy, red straw sunhat drooped fashionably over her face. 'How's the portrait going, Nonno?' she asked, smiling at him indulgently as she sashayed over and dropped a kiss on his forehead.

'Look for yourself,' he invited, smiling at Jenny. 'I think you'll have to credit Bella with more talent than you had imagined, Lucia.'

'Really?'

The incredulous tone in her voice instantly made Jenny bridle. It was difficult to care about a person who was bent on being critical. She felt herself tensing as Lucia moved around to stand behind her and examine the likeness to Dante. She tensed even more when Lucia started laughing.

'You're going to love this, Dante. It's the most romantic version of you anyone could turn out.'

'Romantic?' he queried, looking at Jenny in a bemused fashion.

'I guess that's what street artists do, try to please the person they're drawing,' Lucia rattled on mockingly. 'Never mind about their true character, which, of course, they don't have a clue about. Though I must say, Bella, you should have picked up some of Dante's by now. You've been with him long enough.'

A horrible flush of self-consciousness flooded up Jenny's neck as she stared at the portrait, realising she had poured her feelings into it, making his eyes more gentle and loving than they really were, giving his mouth the kind of sensuality that reeked of sexual promise.

'Where's his master-of-the-situation arrogance?' Lucia demanded. 'The cutting-edge cynicism? All those innate qualities that make him such a force to be reckoned with?'

'I obviously don't know him so well,' Jenny

muttered, shooting an anxious look at Marco. 'I'm sorry if you're disappointed.'

'Not at all, my dear. I'm glad Dante has shown you the softer side of himself.' He held out his hand. 'If you've finished, let me see it more closely.'

Jenny stood to pass over the portrait, achingly aware that Dante had stood, too, and was coming over to view it with his grandfather. Would he be amused to see himself *romanticised* by her? Or would his sharp mind pick up the fantasy of a dream lover that her subconscious self must have been weaving as she drew? Her insides writhed with the humiliation of revealing what should have been kept hidden.

He looked.

He said nothing.

His gaze remained lowered, fixed on the portrait. There was no telling expression on his face.

'I like it,' Marco said in a gruff, wistful tone. 'I like it very much.'

'Then Bella should do one of me, too,' Lucia said petulantly, annoyed by her grandfather's warm approval of Jenny's work.

'She might not see you as you would like to be seen, Lucia,' Dante tossed at her dryly.

'If she can do such a romantic version of you, she can do the same for me. Then Nonno can have the best of both of us to look at,' she argued, flouncing over to the chair Dante had vacated at the table, seating herself in an exaggerated pose, waving a command at Jenny. 'I'm all yours, Bella. Let's see what you can make of me.'

'Where are your manners, Lucia?' Marco asked sharply.

She flashed a saccharine smile at Jenny. 'Pretty please. As a gift to Nonno.'

'I'll do my best,' Jenny hastily agreed, grateful for the distraction from Dante and his reaction to the portrait she'd done. Besides, if she 'romanticised' Lucia, he would think that was her style, nothing personal to him.

She sat herself at the easel again, picked up a stick of charcoal and began drawing, emptying her mind of the spite and jealousy that soured Lucia's character, trying to see her as a lost child who was still occupying a frighteningly empty world, wanting the love she had missed.

Dante stretched out on another sun-lounge, remaining quiet as Lucia babbled on to her grandfather, telling him of the call she'd taken from her mother this morning. Apparently Sophia was waiting for her brother, Roberto, to join her in Paris before both flew down to Capri for the weekend to visit their father and meet Bella. Jenny hoped her pseudo aunt and uncle were not going to put her through any hostile hoops while they were here.

She listened to Lucia's rambling on about her family, knowing that meeting the rest of the Rossinis was inevitable. It was only natural they would want to spend time with Marco before he died. Bella might not be a welcome addition to the scene at this late juncture, but they would have to accept her presence.

It would be interesting to see how they responded to Dante, being the person designated to take over from Marco. Did they resent him as Lucia did, or were they content for him to carry the responsibility of the family fortunes?

Not that it was any of her business. She had to remain apart from all family politics. This wasn't her life. It was simply time out of time.

'I'm done,' she told Lucia, silently vowing not to let this 'cousin' upset her again. Since the portrait had been requested for Marco, she took it off the easel and handed it to him. 'Your gift,' she said with a smile.

'Thank you,' he murmured, staring at her work as his two real grandchildren moved to satisfy their curiosity about it.

Again Dante said nothing.

Lucia rushed into a string of protests. 'This isn't what you did for Dante. The eyes are too dark and intense. They should be bright and happy. You've made me look edgy instead of romantic. I don't like it.'

Jenny shrugged off the criticism. 'I'm sorry it doesn't meet your expectations. I'll try again another day if you want me to.'

'I wanted Nonno to have it today.'

'No, Lucia,' Marco said firmly, shooting her a quelling look. 'I'm satisfied with this one and Bella has indulged us enough. It's ungracious of you to demand more.'

'But, Nonno…'

'Enough!' he repeated sharply. 'I want you and Dante to leave me with Bella now. I'm tired and I'd like a few minutes alone with her before Theresa wheels me off to bed.'

'Then I'll go back to the pool. You can join me there later, Bella,' Lucia tossed at her with a show of cousinly grace as she left them.

Dante moved to pack up the easel. 'I'll take this back to your suite, Bella,' he said, his eyes stabbing a command for her to join him there when his grandfather was finished with her.

'Theresa, go and look at the sea,' Marco instructed, waving towards the cliff wall, obviously wanting his caregiver out of earshot, as well.

Tension streaked along Jenny's nerves as she waited for the private tête-à-tête Marco was intent upon. This would be another test she had to pass, completely on her own this time. Fatigue was drawn on the old man's face but it hadn't dulled the sharp intelligence in the eyes he turned to her.

'You are a very talented artist, Bella. No question about that,' he said with authority.

'Thank you.' She smiled at the compliment, hiding her angst over what questions he *did* have in his mind.

'Sensitive to your subjects,' was his next comment.

The probe in his eyes made Jenny squirm inside. She was too frightened to say anything in case she revealed even more than she had done already with her unwitting interpretation of Dante.

Marco still held both portraits in his hands and he spread them apart, studying them again before quietly stating. 'These speak to me. I don't know if you meant them to…' Again the sharp probe, striking at her heart, making it flutter with fear. '…and perhaps they tell me more about you than they do about Dante and Lucia.'

'No, no…' She shook her head, her mind frantically searching for a defence of what she'd drawn. 'You asked me for a portrait of Dante, and what I do know about him, with absolute certainty, is that he loves you very much. I tried to show it.'

He nodded, but she wasn't sure he completely accepted her explanation.

'Love…yes,' he murmured. 'Thank you, my dear. It's good to be reminded.'

Relief coursed through her. He wasn't going to attach it to anything personal in her. His gaze moved to the other portrait.

'You've captured something quite different in Lucia.'

'I didn't mean to suggest she doesn't love you,' Jenny said quickly, hoping she hadn't hurt the old man.

He shook his head, a wry twist on his mouth. 'I doubt Lucia is capable of loving anyone. She thinks of herself too much.'

'Is that her fault?' The words were out before Jenny could think better of the criticism they implied. She immediately tried to mitigate them. 'From what Lucia told me last night, she's had a difficult life, having to change schools and go wherever her mother wanted to go. She never had the kind of relationship Dante had with you. I think she's a very unhappy person.'

'Yes.' He heaved a deep sigh. 'It is unfortunate. If my Isabella had still been alive to guide Sophia into being a better mother...more consistent in her caring for Lucia...' He grimaced. 'And Sophia's husbands have been worthless as fathers. Bad choices.'

His eyes sought her understanding. 'I have done all I could for Lucia, offered her every opportunity to make her life count for something other than the wealth attached to her name. She chooses to be a dilettante, and while she sticks to that course, she will not attain any inner happiness. I can't make her change. And be warned, my dear, she will tear your sympathetic heart to shreds, seeing it as a weakness to be exploited.'

'Why? I thought she felt lost. Like no one ever cared enough about her,' Jenny pleaded. 'I'm sorry if that's presumptuous, but—'

'No. Lucia is very clever at painting the pictures she wants to present. Which is whatever will suit her purpose at the time. Care was certainly lavished on her when she was a little girl, but even then it was in her nature to destroy rather than build something good. She is not a lost child, Bella, more an *enfante terrible* who enjoys wreaking havoc.'

'Because she wants more notice taken of her?'

Jenny suggested, still reaching for more understanding of what sounded like psychotic behaviour.

'To make herself the centre of attention, yes. But not to care about the effect of her actions on anyone else. She has long had a habit of engineering situations that give her a destructive control. I have come to believe this behaviour stems from a personality disorder, perhaps a genetic inheritance from her father who had no conscience at all. I don't know. I only see how it is. But Lucia is family and I will never again turn my back on family. When I'm gone it will be Dante's responsibility to look after her, see to her needs as best he can.'

Jenny frowned over what she saw as an extremely strained relationship between the two cousins. 'Surely her mother should do that.'

'Oh, I'm sure Lucia will milk the guilt trip she loads on Sophia for all she can, but Dante will hold the reins on how much is given. He knows where to draw the line, and draw it he will with authority that cannot be bucked.'

As he had already done twice since she had been here. But would he be as tolerant as his grandfather when he was left in charge of the family? 'You trust him with a great deal,' she said musingly.

'He has earned my trust a thousand times over. Not once has he ever let me down.'

Nor would he at the end of Marco's life, Jenny thought, feeling more sympathetic towards the deception Dante had enforced. His grandfather had sent him on an impossible mission and she had been the answer to it.

'I think it must be very rare…what you and Dante share,' she said in wry appreciation.

'Yes. As rare as finding the love of a good woman. I have been fortunate with my wife and my grandson. And I'm glad he found you, my dear, and brought you home with him.'

Embarrassed by the linkage to people who

were truly dear to Marco, Jenny muttered, 'I had to come. But please don't feel you have to do something for me. Just being here is enough.'

'I hope it will be.'

His smile was so benevolent, Jenny wished she was his grand-daughter. It would be so nice to belong to him.

'Thank you for the portraits, my dear. And don't let Lucia spoil your stay here. Dante will keep you company when I can't. Trust him to deal with any situation that arises. Will you do that?'

She nodded, acutely aware there was too much family history she didn't know.

He waved a dismissal. 'Time for me to retire. Will you tell Theresa I'm ready to go?'

'Of course. I hope you have a good rest.'

Having taken her leave of Marco, she strolled along the cliff walkway which would take her to her suite, looking out at the deep blue sea and thinking over all he had told her. Patterns of behaviour did reveal the person. Lucia only wanted Marco's attention when he was giving it to others. 'Bella' wasn't taking up what could have been her time with him. Lucia only wanted it to take it away from Bella. Or Dante. Not to use it for anything that might be good and meaningful.

Don't let her spoil your stay here.

I won't, Jenny resolved.

Which left only Dante weighing on her mind—Dante, whom she now saw waiting for her outside her suite—Dante, propped casually against the stone wall, watching her with a dark intensity that sent little quivers through her entire body.

Her feet faltered to a halt.

She burned with embarrassment, remembering the 'romantic' portrait. Love had nothing to do with what he'd done with her last night. He wanted to keep her here for his grandfather, by any means—a ruthless manipulator. Her head told her that, but her heart…her heart was drowning in a deep blue sea, beating against conflicting waves of emotion that could not be held at bay.

CHAPTER THIRTEEN

DANTE saw her leisurely stroll along the walkway come to an abrupt halt when she caught sight of him waiting for her. The pensive look on her face instantly changed—a self-conscious flush bursting onto her cheeks, a tense defensiveness in the sharp tilt of her chin, wariness in the eyes that met his—and he knew without a doubt that she had exposed her heart in the portrait of him. In both portraits, but the one of Lucia did not concern him so personally.

His conscience had been pricking him from the moment he took in what she had drawn. It wasn't the man he'd been to her. If she'd portrayed what she wanted him to be, he'd taken too many liberties with the person she was, been blindly selfish in going after what he wanted, not giving any thought to how his actions would affect her, except in so far as they achieved his purpose.

His sense of righteousness over using her had received one hell of a hard knock. He'd known she was vulnerable, and he'd exploited her vulnerability, telling himself the end justified the means. He'd overlooked the fact that she had been an abandoned child whose need to be loved and cherished had never been answered. It had only been sex to him last night, but if she had fantasised love, she could end up deeply hurt by her connection to him.

This wasn't a woman he could kiss off with some lavish gift when the mutual pleasure wore thin. He knew she would be insulted, mortally offended, believing he truly had used her as his 'secret little whore.' Jenny Kent was essentially a good person, not wanting to do harm to anyone. It was in her every word, every action.

He'd known it last night. She was a giver, not a user.

He shouldn't keep taking from her.

Yet he couldn't bring himself to tell his grandfather the truth—that Bella was dead and he'd brought Jenny Kent in her place to ease the guilt and pain over his lost son. Nonno wanted her here. He liked her. It was helping him get through this bad time.

Apart from which, Dante wanted Jenny Kent to stay for himself. Desire for her was burning through his body right now, urging him to dismiss his concern over how deeply she was responding to him. He wasn't *forcing* her to have sex with him. It was her choice. She had made that clear to him last night. *Her choice...*

Yet his instincts were telling him this was not the time to push for the physical satisfaction of having her again. It had been a pressure morning for her and she probably needed space to herself—a rest from the inner conflict of having to be Bella. On the other hand, if he gave her room to think too much, her mind might be torn over the deception again. What had his grandfather said to her after he had dismissed Lucia and himself?

Her shoulders straightened and she pushed her feet forward again. Dante sensed a proud refusal to be intimidated by anything he thought or said. Jenny Kent made her own way, regardless of the forces she had to contend with—a survivor, no matter what. He had to admire her spirit. In fact, there was nothing he didn't admire about her. She was a beautiful woman, inside and out.

'I didn't break your trust,' she assured him, once she was standing at the stone wall, close to his position but not in touching distance. Her lovely amber eyes looked directly into his to drive the point home. 'Your grandfather still thinks I'm Bella.'

Which was why she was here.

Dante got the message.

Having sex with him was a side issue, not the

main event, and whatever it meant to her was not to be discussed. It would happen—if it did again—behind closed doors and that was where Jenny Kent would leave it when her life moved on beyond this time on Capri. Dante told himself he should be feeling relief at her attitude. It freed him from any guilt over treating her too cavalierly. Yet for some unfathomable reason, he didn't like her return to rigid self-containment. He wanted her. He wanted *all* of her.

Maybe it was the lure of forbidden territory.

The challenge she continually posed.

Whatever…now was not the time to pursue it.

'What did he want to talk to you about?' he asked.

'Lucia mostly. He wanted me to understand her personality so I wouldn't get too upset by anything she did or said.'

To Dante's mind, that underlined his grandfather's need to keep Bella here. 'Nonno well knows her penchant for creating scenes when she's not getting her own way,' he commented, nodding to himself. 'Lucia has been quite a malicious little manipulator all her life.'

'You're not too backward at manipulation yourself, Dante,' she shot at him, a weighing look in her eyes as though she was measuring his integrity.

'My actions are never motivated by malice,' he stated unequivocally.

'But you are ruthless when it comes to executing your vision of the greater good. And cynical in your judgement of people. Lucia was right in pointing that out to me.'

'Lucia's aim is to divide and conquer. She doesn't want us to be close. The more she can drive a wedge between us the better she'll like it.'

'I'm not stupid, Dante. I know that staying close to you is my best chance of holding all this together. I need your support and protection and I trust you to give me both. But I'm well aware of when our togetherness will come to an end, so please don't think I'll fool myself into getting *romantic* about you. Your grandfather wanted a portrait of you. I gave him a loving one.'

She spoke coolly, but her eyes hotly denied any other interpretation of what she'd drawn. Pride, he thought, and an array of conflicting emotions coursing through the pragmatism she had persistently demonstrated since he'd forced her into this situation. The problem was that the mind could see a logical reality and accept it, but how the heart reacted to it was not so easily governed.

'Thank you for using your artistry to give me such a kind treatment,' he said quietly, feeling an odd spurt of tenderness for this woman who cared so much. 'It was very generous of you. Nonno was touched by it.'

She sucked in a deep breath and managed a shaky smile. 'He did like it. I should have done the same for Lucia instead of annoying her by portraying her differently.'

'It was, I thought, a sympathetic portrait of her,' he posed, wondering if she would shield herself against Lucia's poisonous darts or suffer from them.

She shrugged as the smile turned into a rueful grimace. 'Don't worry. Anything Lucia says to me will be water off a duck's back from now on. She's your business, not mine.'

'A cross I have to bear,' he said dryly. 'And speaking of Lucia, do you want to brave a swim in the pool while she's there?'

Out in the open where she could please herself—swim, laze in the sun or shade, chat or flip through the magazines Lucia always had handy—a place to relax, Dante thought, and regather herself, without any push for more intimacy from him. He could almost see the same train of thought going through her mind before a smile of relief spread across her face.

'Yes. A swim would be good.'

He nodded agreement. 'I'll meet you at the pool.'

Which took away any fear he might invade her room while she was getting changed.

The smile brightened. 'Okay! See you there!'

She left him with an eager bounce in her step—the bounce of freedom from expectations she wasn't up to facing right now. He had kept her on a tight rein, intent on covering every problem that could arise from the situation. The most critical time had already been successfully negotiated. She was doing really well in the role of Bella, better than he had ever anticipated. It was time to loosen up, give more consideration to Jenny Kent's needs.

Dante wondered if he should keep away tonight.

Did she want him to?

That was the more pertinent question.

Jenny actually enjoyed the time they spent in and out of the pool. Lucia was with them which ensured Dante acted in a cousinly manner, affably fetching them drinks when requested, making occasional droll comments on the conversation about fashion in different countries, which Lucia kept rolling as she leafed through magazines.

Jenny had very little experience of designer-wear—only what Dante had acquired for Bella—but her general ignorance didn't matter. Lucia enjoyed being the expert, showing off all her inside knowledge of the subject, gossiping about top models with whom she was personally acquainted. It obviously made her feel superior to her Australian cousin and that was fine. Nothing really nasty was said. Dante's presence was undoubtedly an inhibiting factor on that front.

Certainly neither cousin was the least bit inhibited about exposing their bodies. The bottom half of Lucia's red bikini was virtually a G-string and so was Dante's swimming costume which was not much more than a black pouch, forming a tantalising magnet for Jenny's eyes. She continually had to make a conscious effort not to keep looking *there*. As it was, the rest of his magnificent physique was more than enough to flood her mind with memories of last night's intimacy.

It made her doubly conscious of her own body. She wore a more modest bikini in a pretty apple green, a Zimmerman design featuring feminine little frills on the side of the bra and across her hipline, bought by Dante but chosen by her. She felt comfortable in it, except when *his* gaze roved over her. Several times she was driven back into the pool to reduce the heat of wanting this man too much.

She knew it wasn't sensible.

But the sexuality he'd stirred in her had a life of its own, pulsing a constant rebellion against any common sense.

When would she ever meet a man like him again—a man who could make her feel like this?

Most probably never.

As long as she kept in her head, there would

be no happy-ever-after with him, why not take whatever he gave of himself? She wanted it, more than anything she had ever wanted. If he came to her tonight…but that was hours away and she had to keep cool in front of Lucia. Cool to him, too, because she didn't want him to know how besotted she was becoming with him.

The three of them had a leisurely lunch beside the pool. Jenny concentrated hard on enjoying the food—delicious Atlantic salmon served with a scrumptious side salad containing wedges of sweet orange and roasted pecan nuts. Fresh fruit was served afterwards; little balls of different melons and pineapple sprinkled with mint. They drank a lovely refreshing white Italian wine which was so pleasant to the palate, she drank too much of it, ending up feeling so drowsy, she was glad when Dante announced it was time for a siesta.

He accompanied her back to her suite, maintaining a relaxed manner as they walked along. Jenny was careful not to reveal any sexual tension, asking questions about Italy and showing interest in his answers. He left her at her door, casually moving on to his own suite, and she wondered if he had decided not to get too entangled with her.

Had the portrait suggested to him a risk of emotional attachment that might cause problems for him further down the line, problems he didn't want to deal with?

It was no use worrying about it, Jenny told herself. She'd done her best to tell him she knew the score where their relationship was concerned. What Dante chose to do about it was beyond her control. *He* was the controller, of every sphere in his life. It was so imbued in his character, Jenny couldn't imagine him any other way.

She took a long, cool shower to reduce her body heat, decided not to wash her hair until after siesta, and had just wrapped herself in a towel when she heard a knock on the door that linked their suites. For a few moments she dithered over answering it. Should she pretend to be already asleep? Had he heard her shower running? What did he want?

Her heart was suddenly pounding in her chest, thundering in her ears. She was acutely conscious of her nakedness under the towel—less naked than in her bikini, yet more instantly available if sex was on his mind. Her body felt like a mass of zinging nerve ends, urging her to go to the door, open it, find out where she was with him.

She did.

He, too, wore only a towel. It was tucked around his waist. She stared at his bare, beautifully muscled chest, the satin-smooth olive skin stretched tightly over it, her hands itching to touch, to feel him as she had felt him last night. It took an act of will to lift her gaze to his and project an innocent inquiry.

The dark eyes blazed raw desire at her. 'Do you want to be alone?' he asked.

A simple question but they both knew it wasn't simple.

It carried an undertow of danger which could sweep them away from any safe ground.

She knew he would force himself to clamp down on his rampant sexual need to have her again if she said yes. The determined restraint he was holding screamed of almost unbearable tension, and something deeply primitive in her revelled in the fact that he had been driven to this door, probably against his better judgement.

The decision was hers to make.

Her mind had already made it.

'No,' she said.

And didn't care where it led for her…further down the track. Regardless of what pain it might bring, she would take the pleasure now.

CHAPTER FOURTEEN

Six weeks passed…. For Jenny, the days blurred into each other, the pattern of them only broken by visits from Uncle Roberto and Aunt Sophia each weekend, both of whom accepted her as Bella without question. Their curiosity about her was easily satisfied and they weren't the least bit concerned about having a late addition to the family getting attention from their father.

Regret was expressed over Antonio's unfortunate death. They would have liked to meet him again. 'He was a terrible scallywag in his youth,' Sophia remarked, which Roberto had hastily discounted with, 'No, no, he was a darling boy,' smiling kindly at his new niece. As far as they were concerned, if it pleased Papa to have her here, it was good that she had come.

Perhaps it also took some emotional pressure off them. They were uncomfortable in the face of Marco's physical decline. Sophia's rather brittle personality was prone to gushing tears over her father. Roberto would set out to amuse—too anxiously—then fall into a glum silence. Jenny felt Marco suffered their visits, trying to soothe their distress when they were with him.

They looked to Dante to take care of everything. There was certainly no resentment of his designated position as the future head of the family. It was obvious they had no wish to carry the load, and Jenny noted that Dante treated them gently, like fretful children whom he knew were incapable of coping with any heavy responsibility.

He was The Man.

In every respect, Jenny thought, having long lost her resentment over his dominating strength of mind and purpose. Not many people had the force of will to do what had to be done, and he didn't use his power without any sense of caring. She'd seen the caring in action, felt it for herself, and understood why his grandfather had placed so much confidence in him.

Only with Dante was Marco completely relaxed. Lucia he more or less indulgently tolerated because she never showed any sign of being unhappy about his dying. As for herself, Marco indulged himself with her, reliving memories that encompassed his whole life, not just the part that was centred on his lost son.

Conversations with him were not the strain she had expected them to be, particularly whenever he insisted that Dante or Lucia leave them alone together. He didn't question her about Antonio's life in Australia which she would have found difficult, and she enjoyed listening to his memories: his boyhood and family background, meeting his Isabella and the life they'd had together, how he'd built up his huge business empire, the hotels, the forums, the pride he took in them, the pride he took in Dante, who would carry what he'd built into the future, not waste it.

'A good boy…'

She didn't know how many times she heard that phrase, always imbued with love and approval. She grew genuinely fond of the old man and felt sorry for the life that was slipping away—a remarkable life, fully lived in so many ways. Sometimes he patted her hand, saying she was, 'A good girl,' making her wish she *was* his grand-daughter.

Though, she was glad there was no blood relationship when she was alone with Dante. They spent siestas and the nights together, pleasuring each other, and it wasn't only hot, urgent sex. She loved the physical intimacy of simply being held close to him, going to sleep in his arms, the mental intimacy of being locked into a secret world of their own.

Quite often they talked late into the night, she relating things his grandfather had told her, he elaborating on them, connecting them to the life he'd shared with Marco. She told him things about her own life she'd never confided to anyone, even about the nasty clash with the sleazy welfare officer. Somehow it didn't matter that he knew. This was time out of time, and once it was over, nothing she said to him would come back to hurt her. The one thing she wasn't open about was how much her heart had filled with loving him.

Occasionally she worried that Lucia was suspicious about how close they were—unguarded moments when a look or a comment revealed an intimacy that shouldn't be there, not between cousins. She grew more and more conscious of Lucia watching, making snide little remarks about how amazingly occupied Dante was with her company, how considerate he was to her needs—taking her off to various parts of the island for her to paint pretty landscapes, staying with her while she did them—and how incredibly well they clicked when they talked.

'Anyone would think you were lovers,' she tossed off one morning while they were lazing on lounges by the pool, her keen bright eyes sharply observing their response.

It was impossible for Jenny to stop a tide of heat from racing into her cheeks.

'You're embarrassing Bella again, Lucia,' Dante rolled out with an air of impatience over her pretend playfulness. 'I promised Nonno I'd look after her as best I could and I'm grateful that Bella is making it easy for me. Which is something you rarely do.'

'No fun in that, dear cousin,' she flipped back at him.

He glowered a warning. 'Don't inflict your brand of fun on Bella.'

'Big Brother is watching,' she intoned in a robotic voice, her eyes merrily mocking him.

'Nonno asked me to,' he said, as though he was simply fulfilling a duty of care.

Lucia smiled sweetly. 'Well, Little Sister is also watching, Dante, and one day…one day you'll slip up and I'll get the better of you.'

He shrugged. 'A rather petty aim in life.'

'But, oh, so satisfying,' she drawled, relaxing back on her lounge with a smug air.

Dante brushed off the incident as just another gambit from Lucia to make mischief, wanting to discomfort Jenny into being less responsive to him. Still, it made her more wary of how she acted in front of Lucia and only truly relaxed in his company when they were alone together.

Marco grew too weak to leave his bedroom suite. Visits to him were necessarily brief. He was in bad pain and his doctor organised a morphine drip, monitored by shifts of nurses to ensure he had twenty-four-hour care. Warned that the end was near, Dante immediately notified

Sophia and Roberto to come to Capri and be on hand for their father's last days.

My last days, too, Jenny thought, but she couldn't wish for Marco to suffer any longer than he had to. Nor did she speak of *the end* to Dante, knowing he drew comfort from having her to come to at night. The imminent loss of his beloved grandfather weighed heavily on his heart. Being with her was helping him through a bad time, and Jenny refused to spoil one precious moment with him by bringing up what could wait until there was no longer any need for her to be Bella.

The role did not worry her anymore. Dante had been right. It didn't hurt anyone, and Marco had liked having her here—someone with whom he could recount his life, dwelling on what had been good for him. She had served him well and had no regrets over anything she'd done.

The morning of Sophia's and Roberto's expected arrival came. Dante left her bed to return to his own suite and get ready for the day—one that was sure to be harrowing for him, Jenny thought, having to handle his aunt's and uncle's emotions, as well as his own. She watched him walk towards the door that linked their suites, hoping she could take some of the burden off his broad shoulders, make herself available to be sympathetic company.

She had thrown off the bedclothes and was heading for her own bathroom to get ready for the day when he opened the connecting door. He stepped inside his suite, and Lucia's voice rang out in gleeful triumph.

'Got you!'

Jenny froze in her tracks, shock ripping through her.

Lucia was in Dante's bedroom.

He was naked, coming from her suite.

His voice cracked out in anger. 'What the hell are you doing here?'

Then he slammed the door shut behind him,

protecting her, but Jenny knew, knew as sickeningly as the nausea that rolled through her, that Lucia would revel in telling Marco that Dante was sleeping with his cousin. Never mind if the shock of it killed him. Lucia would not deny herself the pleasure and satisfaction of taking Dante down in his grandfather's eyes before he died.

Dante glared at Lucia, his mind scrambling to grapple with the situation, knowing she would make capital out of it. Was there a price he could pay—anything she'd take to keep quiet about it and let Nonno die in peace?

She rolled off the top of his pristine bed—the bed he obviously hadn't slept in—and bounced to her feet, her face alight with malicious delight. 'I paid Nonno an early-morning visit and he asked me to fetch you, Dante. I knocked on your door but you didn't answer so I came in to wake you up.'

He'd forgotten to lock his door. Stupid oversight! And he should have stayed in his room, given that Nonno might want him at his side. No excuse that he had wanted to be with Jenny.

'Better get dressed,' Lucia mockingly advised him, heading for the door she'd left ajar. 'I don't think Nonno will appreciate the *naked* evidence that you've seduced his precious Australian grand-daughter into sleeping with her first cousin.'

'Wait!' he commanded, needing to stop her, to reason with her.

She scuttled the rest of the way to the door, hanging onto it for a moment to throw back at him, 'Oh, I can't wait to tell Nonno what you've been up to.'

'Lucia, don't!' he shouted at her, galvanised into action, wanting to grab her, shake some sense into her.

She laughed as she leapt into the corridor and shut the door in his face. By the time he wrenched it open again, she was running, putting distance between them too fast for Dante to catch her before she reached their grandfather's suite. Even if he did, he knew she would make a scene, and with him stark naked…

No. He had to get dressed, present himself to Nonno as fast as he could with a measure of calm dignity, minimise the damage. His mind jagged to Jenny. She must have heard Lucia. She'd be in shock, worried sick about this outcome from their intimacy. But he didn't have time to go to her. Nonno had to come first.

Clothes on, hair combed, mind tumbling through replies to Lucia's accusations, heart pumping hard as he strode towards a showdown he'd been unable to avoid. The door to his grandfather's suite was open. He could hear Lucia reeling off a string of outrage, pretending to be appalled at his moral transgression.

'Having sex with his first cousin…it's disgusting, Nonno. Incestuous.' She loved rolling out that word. 'Dante has no morals at all. He has the arrogance to believe he can get away with anything. You have to—'

'No!' Dante thundered as he stepped into the room, jolting Lucia into turning to him.

'You can't order me around, you dirty beast!' she jeered.

'You've said your piece. Now get out.'

'I will not.' She folded her arms in defiant righteousness. 'I'm not going to let you lie your way out of this.'

'I have no intention of lying.' He shot an anxious look at his grandfather, who, surprisingly, did not appear to be upset or agitated, his wasted body lying completely still, his dark sunken eyes regarding Dante with the same trust he'd always shown. No shock in them at all.

Did he think Lucia had been lying?

'Leave me with Dante, Lucia,' he commanded in a wheezy whisper.

She instantly wheeled to him in protest. 'But, Nonno…'

'You heard him. Go!' Dante cut in fiercely, advancing on her, prepared to throw her out bodily if she refused to move.

'Go…' their grandfather weakly echoed.

Lucia huffed her displeasure at this second dismissal. She hated missing the fun, but had to accept that she couldn't push her presence any further. 'I've told you the absolute truth, Nonno. It's only right that you know what he's really like,' was her parting shot as she flounced to the door.

Dante shut it behind her, knowing she would eavesdrop if she could. He wouldn't give her *that* satisfaction. It was impossible to pretend that she had been lying, impossible to betray the trust in his grandfather's eyes, though he had been betraying it these past two months, presenting Jenny as Bella, maintaining the fiction. He couldn't do it anymore, not now at the end.

He sucked in a deep breath, walked over to the chair at his grandfather's bedside, drew it close, sat down, reached out and took his hand, pressing it gently, his eyes begging for understanding as he said, 'I'm sorry, Nonno.'

The almost skeletal hand squeezed back. There was no criticism in his eyes, no judgement, only trust. 'No need…for apology.'

'There's a lot I must tell you.'

'No…only one thing.' He struggled for more breath.

Dante waited, his mind racing in search of the one thing his grandfather wanted to know—the one thing that was more important to him than all of Lucia's vitriolic accusations.

He wasn't expecting the question that came. He hadn't ever asked it of himself. Nor had Jenny. It completely bypassed the deception they had played and bored straight into his heart. A simple question, loaded with the implicit demand for a truthful answer.

'Do you love her?'

CHAPTER FIFTEEN

JENNY stopped her fretful pacing at the sound of the connecting door being opened. Was it Dante or Lucia? Driven by the frightened need to hide her own nakedness and look presentable, she'd thrown on some clothes, pushed her feet into sandals, brushed her hair into reasonable order, and tried to apply some makeup, though her hands had been shaking too much to attempt more than basic stuff. She had no idea how many minutes had passed since Lucia had confronted Dante in his bedroom, but her heart was still racing so hard, her hand instinctively lifted to cover its wild beat as she whirled to face whoever came into her room.

Dante!

She sagged with relief.

Though the relief was short-lived.

His grim face told her he'd been unable to stop Lucia from doing her worst, running to his grandfather with the news that they were lovers. Her heart sank. The deception they'd played successfully right up to this eleventh hour had surely come unstuck. Dante could not carry the horrible stigma of sleeping with his first cousin.

'You've been alone, Jenny?' he asked, sharp concern in his eyes as he crossed the room to where she stood.

'Yes.'

'I'm sorry. I'm grievously at fault for not locking my door, allowing Lucia the chance to—'

'Tell me what's happened,' she cut in, only too aware that what was done was done and couldn't be undone.

He drew her into his embrace, held her tightly for a few moments, then eased back, his eyes begging her to understand and support whatever he'd put into place.

'Lucia got to Nonno before I could. She told him I'd been sleeping with you. He ordered Lucia out. He didn't want to listen to any explanations from me. He was concerned about you. He asked me to bring you to him now, Jenny. Can you handle this?'

No escape.

There never had been from the moment Dante had walked into her life.

She was tied to him for as long as he wanted her.

'I'll do my best,' she said.

Worry lines drew his brows together. 'If you'll just give him the answers he wants, Jenny, give him whatever he needs from you…'

'I understand,' she said, trembling inside at the prospect of facing Marco and having to set his mind at rest.

'Thank you. Let's go then. I told the nurse to lock his door and keep Lucia out. He's waiting for us.'

He dropped his embrace and hugged her shoulders as they began to move, assuring her they were together in this, right to the end. He wouldn't abandon her in Marco's room, though what either of them could do there was very much up in the air.

She half-expected to find Lucia lurking along the corridor, revelling in her triumph over Dante, wanting to gauge how much trouble she had caused, but it was empty of any other presence apart from theirs. Tension tore at her nerves as they waited for the nurse to let them in to be with Marco. She fiercely wished there had never been any deception, yet without it, there would not have been this time with Dante. This final hurdle had to be crossed…somehow.

The door opened. Dante ushered her to the chair at Marco's bedside. He stood just behind her, one hand resting on her shoulder in a show of togetherness. His grandfather lay still, his eyes closed, his face so gaunt and grey, her heart instantly went out to the old man who clearly had little time left in this world. He'd always been kind to her and she desperately wanted to treat him with kindness in these last hours of his life.

'I'm here, Marco,' she said softly.

A little smile curved his lips. 'Good girl!' he murmured, then slowly lifted his eyelids, turned his head on the pillow and looked directly into her eyes. 'Now tell me, my dear…who are you?'

For one paralysing moment, she thought he had lost the power to recognise people. Then she realised there was no dulling of intelligence in the knowing dark eyes that sought the truth from her, and shock pummelled her again.

Marco knew she wasn't Bella.

She had no idea when he had come to this conclusion. Maybe he had suspected it from quite early on, given that he had accepted the sketchiest details of Antonio's life in Australia without probing for more. Maybe the fact that she and Dante were lovers had clinched it for him. The grandson he knew so well would not have slept with his first cousin.

A huge sense of relief swept through her as the burden of deception was lifted. She would not be breaking Dante's trust to speak the truth now. He'd asked her to give his grandfather whatever he wanted.

'My name is Jenny Kent,' she said openly and honestly.

They were the words she should have spoken in the hospital when she'd woken up from the coma. Dante's fingers dug into her shoulder with bruising strength. Was he appalled at her confession? It was too late to take it back. Besides, it was right to give up the truth. Marco's eyes told her it was right.

'I was Bella's friend,' she went on. 'Neither of us had family and we became like sisters. I shared her apartment and she lent me her Italian name so I could work in the Venetian Forum. I'm sorry, Marco, but she was the one who died in the car accident, and the authorities mistakenly identified her as me.'

The whole story poured out, from convincing herself that taking on Bella's identity for a while would not harm anyone to Dante's insistence that she come to Capri in Bella's place. '…because he loves you, Marco, and he couldn't bear to tell you Antonio's daughter was dead, too. I hoped I knew enough about Bella's life to…to satisfy you…but I can tell you now—' she leant forward earnestly '—your grand-daughter was a wonderful person, generous and kind, endlessly curious about everything, more fun than I am and I wish she had been alive for you.'

He lifted his hand to wave aside her concern, dragging in breath to speak. 'You…you are more important, Jenny.'

'Me? But I'm no one,' she protested painfully.

'Listen to me…'

The rasping urgency in his voice silenced her. It hurt to watch him summoning the strength to speak, the effort it took to deliver what he wanted to say. All she could do was respect his request for her to listen and hope that Dante wasn't hating her too much for spilling out his part in the deception. Maybe she should have taken all responsibility for it herself, as she had once planned to, but then he would still be guilty of sleeping with a woman he believed to be his first cousin. Better that he hear the truth.

Her heart ached with the knowledge she had just ended her time with him. Jenny Kent had no part to play here. When the helicopter arrived with Roberto and Sophia, it could take her away, out of the Rossini family where she had never belonged, out of Dante's life where she wouldn't belong, either.

Marco wheezed in another deep breath and said, 'I saw your feelings for Dante…in the portrait.'

No, no, no, her mind screamed. She'd tried so hard to hide them. For his grandfather to point them up in front of Dante now…

'I put it together then,' he went on. 'No family likeness…your reticence about Antonio…so many careful reservations…Dante, too watchful…'

So soon, Jenny thought, anguished over being seen as a fraud almost from the very beginning.

'Why didn't you say, Nonno?' Dante asked, his voice gruff with the emotions coursing through him.

Marco's gaze lifted to his grandson. He struggled to reply. 'I wanted her to stay…to observe the connection between you…to see if you would come to feel for her…what I felt for my Isabella. To have a good woman at your side, Dante…sympathetic, strong, caring, sharing. I wished that for you, my boy…more than I wished for a grand-daughter I'd never known.'

Tears welled into Jenny's eyes. This was a dying man's dream, wanting to believe his beloved grandson would be happily settled with a good woman in the future. It wasn't going to happen. Not with her. As much as she would love to be at Dante's side for the rest of her life, she knew his involvement with her was only a *pro temps* thing, bound up in sexual pleasure and secrecy, but she remained silent, unable to bring herself to tell Marco that. It was up to Dante to speak the truth this time.

But he said nothing and Marco reached out to her. 'Give me your hand, Jenny.'

She did, desperately blinking the tears away so she could meet his gaze without blurred vision.

'I want you to know…you've been very good for me.'

The tears welled again. She couldn't stop them.

Marco pressed her hand gently. 'You do love Dante, don't you?'

Such a direct question…Dante's voice in her head, telling her to give the answers his grandfather wanted, his hand squeezing her shoulder again. 'Yes,' she choked out. It was the truth anyway.

Marco's breath whistled out on a long sigh. He

sucked in again. 'Don't waste time, Dante. Marry her soon.'

Marry?

'I will, Nonno,' came the strong promise.

The blank shock in Jenny's mind receded at the quick realisation that Dante was giving the answer Marco wanted to hear.

'In the safe…in my study…give her Isabella's ring.'

'It will honour our commitment to each other. Thank you.' Dante's voice was more furred this time.

'You have my blessing. Both of you.'

He patted Jenny's hand.

She couldn't speak over the huge lump of emotion in her throat.

'You'll always be with us, Nonno,' Dante said.

'Good boy.' A last benevolent smile, then, 'Go now. I must rest…for Sophia and Roberto.'

Dante stepped forward, leaned over and kissed both his grandfather's sunken cheeks. 'Rest easy,' he murmured. 'And thank you for all you have given me.'

The dark eyes he turned to Jenny as he straightened up were shiny wet, pleading eloquently for one last effort from her. She swallowed hard to clear her throat, stood up and kissed Marco as Dante had, pouring her own genuine fondness for the old man into what were probably her last words to him.

'Thank you for letting me be Bella. It made me wish you were my grandfather. And thank you for giving me time with Dante. I will always love you for that, Marco.'

No matter what, she thought.

Dante's arm around her waist scooped her away from his grandfather's bedside, swept her quickly to the door the nurse opened and closed behind them. Once outside in the corridor, he swung her into his embrace, tucking her head into the curve of his neck and shoulder, his chest heaving against hers, his cheek rubbing over her hair as he fought to bring his churning emotions under control.

Jenny held him tightly around the waist, hugging this final closeness to him, wanting him to take comfort from it. At least he now knew her confession had not been a mistake. Marco had wanted it. And what had ensued from it was not her fault. She had carried through what Dante had asked of her, and he would not be holding her like this if he didn't feel a mountain of grateful relief.

'*Dio!*' Lucia's shrill voice rang out again. 'You two are absolutely disgusting! Right outside Nonno's door!'

Dante lifted his head. 'Oh, shut up, Lucia!' he barked at her. 'Jenny is not Bella. She was only pretending to be for Nonno's sake, for my sake. He knows that.'

'Not Bella?'

Jenny turned her head and saw Lucia in a frozen pose of utter incredulity.

'Not Bella,' Dante repeated emphatically.

'Jenny Kent, the woman I'm going to marry. And Nonno has just given us his blessing, so you might as well go away and sulk over your failure to *get me*.'

'Marry!'

Jenny empathised with Lucia's shock. What was Dante thinking to make such a public announcement? He couldn't really mean to marry her, could he?

'You're looking at my future wife, so be careful how you treat her, Lucia.'

The warning was loaded with threat. Dante's emotions were still running high. He dropped his embrace, hugged her shoulders again, and walked her straight towards his meddling cousin. Jenny's own emotions were in chaos. Her mind was clogged, incapable of making sense of anything. Her feet went with him, letting him be the puppet-master again.

'That's the helicopter arriving now,' he threw at Lucia as the distinctive sound came from overhead. 'Go and meet your mother and Uncle Roberto. Jenny and I have other business to attend to for Nonno.'

Lucia's face contorted with rage. 'You…' She threw her hands up in the air in furious exasperation. 'You get away with everything!' Then she spun on her heel and marched off ahead of them, her back rigidly rejecting any congratulations on an engagement she could never have envisaged.

Neither had Jenny. Was Dante now determined on carrying out his grandfather's wishes—his deathbed wishes? He was certainly set on it while Marco was still alive. Maybe afterwards, as well. They reached Marco's study before she could sort through her feelings about what was happening. Dante released her and moved to a painting on the wall, swinging it aside to reveal a safe.

'Stop!' The word croaked from her throat, driven out by a desperate need to understand the situation.

He looked back at her, resolute purpose carved on his face, the dark eyes burning up the distance between them, shooting a debilitating bolt of heat through her, weakening her own resolve. She loved him. She wanted to be with him for the rest of her life. But was this real or just another deception?

'You can't marry me just because your grandfather wants you to, Dante,' she cried.

His chin jerked up as though she had hit him. Aggression flared. It pumped through every stride he took back across the room. Her heart kicked into a gallop as she felt the overwhelming power of the man directed straight at her.

She didn't move.

Couldn't move.

He cupped her face, strong hands holding her captive, his eyes blazing into hers. '*I* want to,' he declared with vehement passion. 'And *you* are not going to run out on me, Jenny Kent.'

It almost killed her to say it but she had to. She would not go along with another deception, not one that involved her whole life. 'It's over, Dante. Your need for me has no basis anymore. Your grandfather…'

'This has nothing to do with my grandfather.'

'Of course it has! You said what he wanted to hear. You asked *me* to say what he wanted to hear.'

'Did you lie, Jenny?' he shot at her point-blank, his eyes drilling hers with such penetrating force, all her insides felt pummelled.

Her mind flew into a chaotic whirl. If she admitted the truth, would he wield it like a weapon, beating her into submission to his will?

His fingers pressed at her temples, demanding entry to her thoughts, feeling the wildly leaping pulse under his touch. 'You said you loved me,' he bored in. 'I don't believe that was a lie. All this time with you…I've felt your love in so many ways, you can't deny it. I won't let you deny it!'

But he hadn't said he loved her. Not once had he said it or even implied it. 'I won't be a puppet wife for you!' she cried in desperate protest. 'I want the man I marry to love me, Dante.'

'You think I don't?' His brows jagged together. His eyes fiercely challenged any disbelief on her part. 'I love everything about you. Mind, heart, body and soul…everything! I love you. I need you in my life. I won't let you go.'

Mind, heart, body and soul… A fountain of joy exploded inside her.

'Now say you love me,' he insisted with riveting intensity. 'I know you do. Say it!'

The words spilled out at his command. 'Yes. Yes, I do.' Yet was love enough? Doubt screeched through her mind. 'But, Dante, I wasn't born to your world. You know I'm not a suitable wife for you.'

'I don't care about your background,' he declared in ruthless dismissal of it. 'I've been with you day and night long enough to know the person you are inside, Jenny. It's the person I want to spend my life with.'

Still she couldn't quite bring herself to accept it. 'You shouldn't judge on what we've shared here. It's not your normal life, Dante. Nor mine,' she pleaded, frightened that their relationship wouldn't stand up under other pressures.

'I told you before. My world is what I make it. What *we* will make it together, Jenny. Trust me. It will be good.'

He spoke with such forceful conviction, her fear wavered. She wanted to trust him, yet if he ever came to see her as a mistake, regretting a decision made in an emotionally fraught moment…

'How can you be so certain it will stay good?' she pleaded, desperately worried that she might fail to meet his expectations of a wife.

There wasn't the slightest glimmer of doubt in his eyes. His whole formidable energy force was focused on making her believe. 'Jenny, at the centre of our marriage will be the love we have for each other. Our life will revolve around that, I promise you.'

He believed what he said. *He* would make it happen. What Dante Rossini set out to do, he did.

Jenny's defensive resistance started to melt. Hope surged into her battered mind. She was a survivor. She could adapt to circumstances. Hadn't she done so umpteen times? So long as Dante loved her, she could make their marriage work, too, do whatever had to be done.

'Are you sure, Dante?' she asked, needing to hear his indomitable confidence once again.

'Yes, my love. Very sure.'

His eyes said, 'Enough talk.'

He dropped his hold on her face, his arms sliding around her, bringing her into the warmth and strength of his love, linking them together, bonding them in the union that their marriage would make firm forever.

He kissed her, and Jenny gave up her heart to him.

With the deepest passion she had ever felt.

With all the love she'd tried to keep bottled up.

With trust in the future they would build together.

And afterwards, she accepted the ring that had been the symbol of Marco Rossini's love for his Isabella. She gazed down at it, understanding how very special a gift it was, representing the faith Marco had that their marriage would be as happy as his had been.

'Do you know what a ruby means?' Dante asked.

She shook her head. It was a magnificent ruby, surrounded by diamonds, probably worth a fortune, and she was silently vowing it would never leave her finger, never be mislaid or lost or stolen from her.

'A priceless love,' Dante said softly. 'I know that's what I have with you, Jenny, and I'll always cherish it.'

She looked up, saw in his eyes the promise of everything she had ever dreamed of in her long years of lonely survival, and knew she was truly blessed. This wonderful, amazing, beautiful man would be there for her, filling the rest of her life with love.

CHAPTER SIXTEEN

Four Months Later

JENNY woke up in the Rossini palazzo in Venice and a happy excitement instantly welled up in her. This was her wedding day. She rolled out of bed to draw the curtains on the long windows. The sun was shining. Venice was shining. She smiled and lifted her hand for the beautiful ruby and diamond ring to shine in the light. Another ring would join it today—Dante's ring—but this one would always be very special.

'Isabella,' she murmured, knowing it was the memory of his beloved wife that had been foremost in Marco's mind when he had sent Dante on his mission to bring Antonio's daughter to him, and it was the memory of their love that had kept Marco silent when he could have rightly de-nounced her as a fraud and sent her packing—the same kind of love he wanted Dante to know and have.

If it had not been for the two Isabellas, grand-daughter and grand-mother, she would never have met Dante. Her life would have moved along a very different path, instead of which, here she was, about to marry the most wonder-ful man in the world. And it was not only a marriage blessed by his grandfather, but happily embraced by the rest of the Rossini family.

Even by Lucia. More or less. Poking her nose into all the wedding arrangements, advising Jenny at every turn, meddling so much Dante had confronted her over such zealous interest, suspecting some hidden agenda designed to spoil the big day.

'I actually quite like your chosen bride, Dante,'

she had loftily declared. 'There's not a bitchy bone in her body. And given the power she obviously has over your life, I have hopes she might show up a few flaws in you that I'll enjoy making use of. But first and foremost, I would find it quite intolerable if the Rossini name was not attached to the most spectacular high-society wedding of the year. It's a matter of family pride. And the only way to downplay your bride being a Cinderella is to highlight your status as a billion-dollar prince, never mind your feet of clay.'

'Maybe you'd like to advise me on what shoes to wear,' he'd answered dryly, deciding Lucia's motives were reasonably free of malicious intent.

Jenny hadn't thought there was any at all. Lucia enjoyed showing off her expertise in creating a social event, enjoyed 'Cinderella's' total ignorance of where to go and what to do. Jenny Kent, who had nothing else to her name, *was* much more to her liking than Bella the cousin, who would have rivalled her own position in the family.

Sophia, also, had closely involved herself with the wedding plans, insisting she take on the role of mother of the bride, since Jenny had no family of her own. She didn't have her daughter's drive for organisation, but fluttered around, being supportive. An ineffective mother, Jenny thought, observing how Lucia imposed her own will on Sophia, who invariably wilted over any decision-making but was always well meaning.

As were Roberto and his partner, Jonathon. They had been having a lovely time refurbishing the palazzo's grand reception room for the wedding party that would follow the marriage ceremony in the cathedral. Apparently Marco had not wanted to be openly faced with his son's gay life, but Dante had no reservations about it, and Roberto was delighted that the family ban had been lifted on Jonathon being with him—his joy in this freedom overflowing into a warm benevolence towards Jenny, seeking her approval of the décor changes they had been making, wanting to please.

All in all it seemed to Jenny that the family had grasped her and Dante's wedding as an affirmation of life moving on after the sadness of losing Marco. Even on the day he died the revelation of her real identity and the news of her engagement to Dante had been a distraction from their grief, and there had also been some solace in knowing that Marco had given his blessing to the marriage and had gone to his final rest in a happy, peaceful state of mind.

He'd seen Isabella's ring on her finger and smiled...his last smile. She and Dante had been with him at the end, Dante holding his hand. She could imagine him smiling in spirit today as Dante took her hand in marriage, and she silently promised him her love for his grandson would be as unwavering as Isabella's had been for him.

The blood-red heart of the ruby glowed at her. A priceless love.

Dante stood in the grand foyer of the palazzo, waiting for his bride to come down the staircase, which was festooned with white ribbons and roses. Roberto and Jonathon were fussing around, assuring themselves that all the floral arrangements in the foyer were as stunning as they should be for when the guests would arrive.

They had already passed approval on the flotilla of black-and-gold gondolas outside, saying that they looked magnificent and the gondoliers splendid in their matching uniforms. The musicians in the lead gondola had also pleased them, perfectly attired in formal black dinner suits and white ties. They had reported that the tenor was in fine voice, entertaining the crowd of spectators lining the canal with love songs while they waited to see the bride and groom.

None of this really mattered to Dante, except

in so far as he wanted Jenny to be happy with everything on their wedding day. He loved seeing her glow with pleasure, her lovely amber eyes lit with joy and love for him. She was so different to all the other women he'd known, so very special. Uniquely special.

He was glad his grandfather had seen that she was the right wife for him, pushing him into realising it before he'd thought of it himself. Though he would have come to it. All along, he had wanted to keep Jenny with him, sharing with her what he could not imagine sharing with anyone else. Not once had he looked ahead to her walking out of his life. She was there for him. Always would be now.

We'll have what you had with your Isabella, Nonno, he thought, a little stab of sadness in his heart that his grandfather couldn't be here to see them wed. But they had his blessing and he'd died content with the outcome of the mission to Australia, not getting to know a grand-daughter but a grand-daughter-in-law who had won his approval in every sense…Jenny, who had done so much good.

Even with Lucia, who seemed to have given up mischief-making these past few months in favour of being Jenny's chief advisor on how to fit in with what was expected of a Rossini in any public arena. He gave her an appreciative smile as she came prancing down the staircase, Sophia in tow, both of them looking fabulous in frilly, fuchsia pink designer gowns and wearing happy grins on their faces.

'We're coming down to get the full effect of the bride making her first appearance,' Lucia announced. 'You only have to cool your heels for another minute or two, Dante.'

'Thank you, production manager,' he said, grinning back at her.

She preened. 'I happen to be good at it.'

'Yes,' he agreed. 'I think you would make a brilliant special events organiser in our hotels, if you ever have a mind to take on such a position.'

One eyebrow arched in surprise. 'You'd let me do that?'

'If you really want it, yes. I can't imagine you not making a great success of it.'

Lucia hated failure as much as he did, and if she did seize this opportunity, it might give her a sense of power that would be constructive instead of destructive.

'I'll think about it,' she said, looking immensely pleased. 'We need to get this wedding right first.' She cast a critical eye over him. 'I have to concede you are star material, Dante, but you are about to be outshone by the bride.'

'As it should be,' he replied.

She laughed and turned to stand beside him, Sophia next to her, Roberto and Jonathon arranging themselves on his other side, all faces uplifted as they watched for Jenny to appear.

His bride…

Love and pride swelled his heart as she came floating down the stairs, a vision of such ethereal beauty in her glorious gown and veil, the need to touch her, to assure himself she was real powered through him. He had to force himself to remain still, let her enjoy this moment in the spotlight—his Jenny, who had struggled to survive with so little in her life. He wanted to give her everything.

As she reached the last stair, he did step forward, holding out his hand to take hers.

'Will I do?' she asked, her lovely eyes twinkling with happy confidence, but if she needed some vocal assurance from him, Dante was not about to fail her.

'Beautifully,' he declared, his voice a husky throb of emotion.

She gave him her hand.

And so much more, Dante thought.

A love that filled his life with a deeper pleasure than he had ever known.

A love that cared about everything he did.

A love that had no price on it.

True love.

And he was absolutely committed to giving it right back to her.

0209 Rom LP

MILLS & BOON PUBLISH EIGHT LARGE PRINT TITLES A MONTH. THESE ARE THE EIGHT TITLES FOR MARCH 2009.

RUTHLESSLY BEDDED BY THE ITALIAN BILLIONAIRE
Emma Darcy

MENDEZ'S MISTRESS
Anne Mather

RAFAEL'S SUITABLE BRIDE
Cathy Williams

DESERT PRINCE, DEFIANT VIRGIN
Kim Lawrence

WEDDED IN A WHIRLWIND
Liz Fielding

BLIND DATE WITH THE BOSS
Barbara Hannay

THE TYCOON'S CHRISTMAS PROPOSAL
Jackie Braun

CHRISTMAS WISHES, MISTLETOE KISSES
Fiona Harper

MILLS & BOON
Pure reading pleasure

MILLS & BOON PUBLISH EIGHT LARGE PRINT TITLES A MONTH. THESE ARE THE EIGHT TITLES FOR APRIL 2009.

ɔ

THE GREEK TYCOON'S DISOBEDIENT BRIDE
Lynne Graham

THE VENETIAN'S MIDNIGHT MISTRESS
Carole Mortimer

RUTHLESS TYCOON, INNOCENT WIFE
Helen Brooks

THE SHEIKH'S WAYWARD WIFE
Sandra Marton

THE ITALIAN'S CHRISTMAS MIRACLE
Lucy Gordon

CINDERELLA AND THE COWBOY
Judy Christenberry

HIS MISTLETOE BRIDE
Cara Colter

PREGNANT: FATHER WANTED
Claire Baxter